HOPE AFLOAT

BOOK SIX IN
THE
PARADISE
SERIES

CAROL ANN COLE C.M.

Hope Afloat
© 2025 Carol Ann Cole CM

Cover design: Rebekah Wetmore, from a photo by Olive McKinnon
Editor: Andrew Wetmore

ISBN: 978-1-998149-79-7
First edition July, 2025

Moose House Publications
2475 Perotte Road
Annapolis County, NS B0S 1A0
moosehousepress.com
info@moosehousepress.com

Moose House Publications recognizes the support of the Province of Nova Scotia. We are pleased to work in partnership with the Department of Communities, Culture and Heritage to develop and promote our cultural resources for all Nova Scotians.

We live and work in Mi'kma'ki, the ancestral and unceded territory of the Mi'kmaw people. This territory is covered by the "Treaties of Peace and Friendship" which Mi'kmaw and Wolastoqiyik (Maliseet) people first signed with the British Crown in 1725. The treaties did not deal with surrender of lands and resources but in fact recognized Mi'kmaq and Wolastoqiyik (Maliseet) title and established the rules for what was to be an ongoing relationship between nations. We are all Treaty people.

Also by Carol Ann Cole

The *Paradise* Series

Paradise
Paradise 548
Paradise on the Morrow*
Paradise d'Entremont Private Investigator*
Around the Corner with Paradise*

Other fiction

Less Than Innocent* (co-author)

Non-fiction

Comfort Heart—a Personal Memoir (with Anjali Kapoor)
Lessons Learned Upside the Head
If I Knew Then What I Know Now
From the Heart (with Deanna Jones)
Learning to Slow Dance with Footprints of Kindness*

*from Moose House Publications

Introduction

The Paradise Series has many loyal supporters, including family, friends and strangers. I believe book #6 requires a bit of an introduction for several reasons, not least because many may have not read all of the books in the series.

Hope Afloat jumps ahead seven years from book #5, *Around the Corner with Paradise*. Hope is now a 25-year-old woman whose life has changed dramatically since she graduated high school and moved to Halifax to attend university and live with her mentor, Doctor Sydney Scott. It is some seven years since you heard Hope ask Ben if he could help her with her goal to learn all she could about forensic science. That was not what Ben was hoping to hear.

Over the past years, Doctor Scott has fallen in love. She just doesn't know it yet.

A character we have heard about, Penelope, the daughter of Doctor Scott, makes her first appearance. Through her life to date, Penelope has learned to trust no one.

Hope Afloat is the first book in the series to have Hope on the cover and facing the camera. She first graced the cover of *Paradise d'Entremont Private Investigator*, walking away from the camera. Even Paradise herself has not yet been on the cover facing her fans.

Hope Afloat is about love and family, life and death, murder and chaos, revenge and rage, careers and changes, romance and new love. You know....the usual.

For family...

Jalen

Lexi

James and Tracey

Hope Afloat

Hope Afloat

1: Stop stalling

Doctor Scott and her protégée were hard at work.

"Sit down, Hope. I need you to stop pacing. I'm going to quiz you on what may or may not be part of your final paper. If you get the answer wrong, now is the time, because I can help you work through finding the correct answer."

"That's easy for you to say, Sydney. Having you as my mentor, along with my mom, is the reason that I am always nervous at exam time. What if I screw something up and it's the very thing you have spent literally hours, if not days, helping me study, understand, and recall as required? You know how I can blank out during orals." Hope spoke in a whisper as she leaned toward Sydney.

"Enough whining, kiddo. We have work to do. If you're ready for your first question, listen up."

Hope was sorry she had worn her heart on her sleeve. She said nothing out loud as Sydney opened her old and very large three ring binder she had affectionately labelled 'Doctor Hope.' Hope could see that the binder was nearly full. A sign, perhaps?

"Hope, my questions are not in the order you will have studied each topic. This might cause you some confusion since, beginning with your first year at university, you will have learned things in a very specific order. But things don't come at you in an orderly manner in real life. I'm only hard on you because I know how hard you want to have a long career as a 'Private Investigator Forensics Lead' or whatever the title is on your new business cards. Don't rush this, Hope. That's when accidents happen."

"Sydney, I'm just going to grab a glass of water and then I'm good to go."

Hope pushed her chair back so she could stand up and make her get-away at least for a minute or two.

"Sit down. In case you missed it, there is a jug of water on the table and we each have an empty glass. Stop stalling."

Sydney gave her young protégée a hint of a smile. She did not receive a hint of a smile in return.

Hope quickly poured herself a glass of water but didn't dare offer to do the same for Sydney. She didn't want to run the risk of being accused of stalling a second time. "Fire away. I'm ready...but not overly confident."

"First question," said Sydney. "Outline responsibilities of the Medical Examiner, and leave nothing out."

"A Medical Examiner, in Nova Scotia, is expected to investigate deaths of individuals who die by accident, by suicide, from criminal violence, suddenly when in apparent good health, when unattended by a physician, in a prison, or in any suspicious or unusual manner. I think that's it." She couldn't read Sydney's expression.

"Think again. Have you left anything out?"

"Did I talk about the cremation thing?" Hope was momentarily lost. "Give me a minute."

As she took a drink of water, Hope finally remembered what she had left out. "I should have concluded that the Nova Scotia Medical Examiner also approves cremations."

"Hope, what is going on in that head of yours today? Your mind is elsewhere, and you're having trouble looking me in the eye."

"I need a break—" Hope was interrupted by Sydney, and she was relieved. She hadn't considered what her next words would be.

"How many breaks do you need in one morning? Can you hang in there until lunchtime, at least? We have so much to cover before your next paper is due, and you know that." Sydney sounded angry. "I'm almost handing you a forensic internship, in my own coroner's offices, but you are not there yet. You have so much more to achieve, Hope. Now pay attention for God sake!"

Nothing could have prepared Sydney for what came next...

2: It's late

Hope felt, for her own sanity, that she had to move out of the mansion and that, perhaps without realizing it, Sydney had handed her the opportunity to exit. She quietly stood and collected her papers, her purse, and her coffee. Always, there had to be coffee.

Moving her chair directly in front of Sydney, Hope sat down and made eye contact. Showing no emotion, she began to share what they both knew had to be said regardless of the difficulty involved.

"Sydney, forgive me for speaking about your personal life as well as your work life, but someone has to say this. Your staff has worked here, out of your home, rather than in your offices downtown since the night you were brutally attacked. Everyone needs to find balance in their own life, and letting them return to their office would be a good place to start. Sydney, years have passed and, for your mental health if nothing else, I think you need to face this. Your team needs to see their leader step back out into the real world. I don't have to tell you this is *not* the real world."

Hope didn't take her eyes off Sydney as she spread her arms wide to make her point. "The brutal rape you endured, the fact that you were beaten beyond recognition, and even multiple surgeries that couldn't give you back your face. This face I'm looking at is close, though, and it's a nice one."

Sydney offered a tiny smile but said nothing. Hope felt it was on her to continue.

"I know you have big plans for me. My mother does, as well. The two women I look up to the most are driving me crazy. I need to walk away from all this daily tutorial stuff. I can't even recall if this is what I want...a life of nothing but work. I need to do this for myself, and if that sounds selfish, I'll have to live with that."

Hope could see that Sydney, too, was packing up. Sydney would retreat to her comfortable sitting room/office that she had personally decorated. That's also where she could enjoy her huge television set. Hope had never seen one that size in her life.

Before Sydney made it to the antique doors that opened to her sitting room Hope felt she owed Sydney more. "I'm sorry for letting you down, but this isn't the end of my education at your hands, I can almost guarantee it. That is, if you are willing to be my one-on-one teacher, with a modified curriculum."

Hope knew she would be smart to stop talking. And she would... soon.

"While mom and I truly appreciate the apartment we have here in your incredible home, mom needs to go home and live with dad. They are married. They should, for the most part, live under the same roof. Mom and I have not talked about any of this, so I would appreciate it if you would give me a few days to regroup and drive down to Cape St Mary and be with my family."

Hope was in tears. Sydney was not.

"I think I will just pack up and head to the Cape tonight. I need some Mavillette beach time."

Seconds before Sydney closed her doors, she spoke. "Hope, it's late. We worked well into the evening so, if I may suggest, get a good night's sleep, and drive home in the morning. Give my love to your family. I won't expect to see you until I see you." She closed the door quickly.

Hope left out the personal part about wanting to move out of Sydney's mansion as well. She wouldn't be able to afford much, but anything that would give her quiet when she arrived home would be perfect.

Paradise, Hope's mother, had written the house rules while they were first-time guests in Sydney's home. At the end of the workday, they would *not* interfere with each other's supper and evening plans unless they had made specific plans to dine together. It was Paradise who had played the 'bad cop' when she realized that, if allowed, Sydney would expect Hope to study and work with her every evening until she could barely keep her eyes open.

Hope had not told her mother how Sydney had modified their daily routine. In no time at all Sydney controlled Hope's time at university by providing a car and a driver to take her to and from classes. She was not to lolly-gag at day's end because her driver was waiting to take her back to the mansion, where she knew Sydney would be waiting, checking the clock, getting more angry by the minute.

Hope had not met one single person in over six years of university, every day all day being followed by being home schooled for all remaining hours in the day. Hope was lonely for a life. A life in which you might stop and talk with another student or, God forbid, waste time having a soda with a classmate after school. Since age eighteen she had been living with the Good Doctor, who had a work ethic all her own. Hope didn't find it a very healthy work ethic and certainly not good for one's mental health. She hadn't mentioned this to Sydney because that would have been seen as wasting time.

Hope realized her not speaking out, and her willingness to daily, hourly spend time studying with Sydney looking over shoulder, were her fault as much as Sydney's. Maybe she could not be faulted at age eighteen, but at twenty-five she owned some of what she had been through.

If she had told her parents. Just one call to her mother or father and she would have been out of there.

3: Stay or run away

Paradise opened the door to a wonderful surprise. She knew she had been very close to convincing Penelope that, once she met her birth mother, she would see and understand that all those terrible things she had been told straight from the mouth of her birth father were lies. All lies.

Penelope loved her parents. Her adoptive parents. She did not want all the drama of meeting Doctor Sydney Scott, whom she would *never* accept as her mother. Her father had located Penelope years before Paradise arrived on behalf of Doctor Scott.

Once Paradise found Penelope, she worked very hard to gain her trust. They met several times with no resolution, but still Paradise pressed on. She felt certain Penelope wanted to meet her mother. Not yet, but one day...

Only two nights earlier, Penelope had knocked on Paradise's front door and asked rather sheepishly if Paradise was sincere when she had said, *You will know when you are ready. I will have a bedroom waiting for you.* "Did you honestly mean what you said, Paradise?"

Paradise could barely hear her because she spoke in such muted tones, and she stood to the side of the outside light so she couldn't be seen clearly. In the moment, she did not trust Paradise and she did not trust herself.

"I don't think I did the right thing by making this trip to the Cape, Paradise, yet I can't seem to turn around and leave. I guess I'm lost in more ways than one."

Paradise grabbed Penelope and hugged her tight. They had not embraced before and she could feel how still, almost stiff, Penelope was standing.

She slowly lowered her arms, as did Penelope. *Baby steps*, thought Paradise. *Baby steps.*

"My dear young girl, you will always be welcome in my home. I didn't see a car drive up...how did you get from Montreal to here? Is there someone else who might like to come in?"

Clearly, she didn't drive, thought Paradise. *She isn't answering any questions either.*

Finally Penelope spoke up, in a whisper. "I'm bone-tired, Paradise. Could I possibly wash up and just go to bed? I will answer all your questions to the best of my ability, but in the morning rather than at this late hour."

"Oh. My. God." said Paradise. "I should not be firing twenty questions at you, and I apologize for my behaviour. Perhaps my manners have gone to bed."

Taking one of two suitcases that Penelope had brought with her, she said, "Follow me to your room. You have an en-suite as well, and everything is all set up for you. You will have total privacy."

Walking into a beautifully decorated bedroom with clean towels in the bathroom, Penelope had to ask. "Whose room is this when I'm not here?"

Paradise smile. "This is my daughter's room. Hope has been living in Halifax for years. That's a long story best left for tomorrow as well. Sadly, Hope rarely comes home, so you don't have to worry about her arriving in the middle of the night."

"I have your word that my birth mother will not drop in for morning coffee, correct?"

Slowly closing the door as she spoke, Paradise said, "Halifax is several hours away and, yes, you have my word that Sydney will not be dropping in for coffee. Perhaps one day you will sit in her beautiful, huge study with her. That, too, is a discussion for another day."

Paradise returned to the living room, where Thomas anxiously waited to learn more. "I didn't introduce you, because Penelope is tired, confused, anxious and undecided whether to stay or to run away. Let's sleep lightly tonight, just in case she needs us for anything."

"You don't think she will try to sneak out during the night, do you?"

"I don't know, but I think not," Paradise said.

4: Please make this a priority

Penelope had taken a bold step, surprising everyone, including herself. Her arrival at Cape St Mary was unexpected. *Paradise seemed shocked, but recovered quickly*, thought Penelope.

She lay wide awake after crawling into Hope's bed. She was bone tired, yet her mind would not let her sleep. *Do I really want to meet Doctor Scott? What kind of money do Paradise and her family have, to be living in such an opulent home? Who needs a home this size? What is Hope like, and does she appreciate this beautiful room, with her own bathroom and space enough in the closet to set both of her bags inside and close the closet door?*

As Penelope struggled to pay her bills every month, sometimes only when they were overdue, it was hard to get her head around what was happening all around her. Never once when Paradise tracked her down, and came back repeatedly, did she appear to be a snob of any sort.

Penelope had long ago decided that anyone who had a life like this life must be a snob, or worse. Her birth father had painted a picture of her mother, Sydney Scott, as an uncaring, spiteful, hateful, and selfish whore. And a snob. Penelope couldn't forget the last words he shouted at her after she dared to broach the topic of meeting her birth mother one day and would he be willing to facilitate that first meeting.

"Good God, woman, are you tone deaf? Have you heard anything I have shared with you? Why would you want to meet your mother and what would you hope to gain? Well...?"

Penelope found the courage to interrupt him. "I pride myself in being honest...totally honest. I'm not sure I believe everything you have told me about Doctor Sydney Scott, my mother. I would rather deal with the facts, if you can do that."

Penelope could see how angry she had made her birth father. Deciding she had nothing to lose, she continued. "Why have you not told me *your* name? You keep saying I should be proud to call you 'father.' That is no longer enough. I will find out! Are you perhaps wealthy yourself, a snob who thinks you are so much better than I am?"

Penelope was talking to his back. With a slam of the door, he was gone.

She wasn't upset about his departure, and she hoped he would never knock on her door again. Only once she had locked her door did Penelope consider what he might have done to harm her in his fit of rage.

In a mere whisper, Penelope mouthed her next thoughts, thinking if she said it aloud, she might fall asleep sooner. Not rational, perhaps, but at this time of night, she was prepared to try anything if it led to sleep prior to dawn.

"Dear God in heaven, have I done the right thing by coming here? Can I really trust Paradise? I know all too well that I have built up an unhealthy hatred for those who have money. Did my father really feed me lies about my birth mother? Even worse, why did I believe everything he said, with no need to verify the facts he presented? God, I know I'm a crying mess, but the good news is that I think I can go to sleep now. If you could have all the answers I need in the morning, I would be grateful. I'll check in with you as soon as I wake up. And, God, I know how busy you are, but please make this a priority. I'll never ask for a favour again if you have some clarity for me during the early morning hours."

Our Father who art in heaven…

5: A change of goal

What kept Hope afloat, in all the mess surrounding her studies and her personal life, was the determination, a conviction, to not let her mother down. She was up and out of Sydney's mansion before anyone stirred. She wanted to be gone when Sydney knocked on her door and offered a cup of coffee, 'and a word.' That's how most mornings began.

Paradise, Hope's mother, always left duplicates of her personal items plus a couple of business suits in their suite of rooms within the walls of Sydney's home. Hope, on the other hand, had made a snap decision to take everything that belonged to her home to her bedroom in the Cape. Just thinking about her lovely bedroom made her want to drive just a bit faster. She missed her 'stuff.'

Unsure if she should take any or all the medical books Sydney had 'given' her during their many hours spent preparing Hope for her *end goal,* she decided to take them all. During the past eighteen hours her end goal had changed. It might change again...and she could always return the books to Sydney if it turned out she did not need them.

Hope's goal had changed *from* wanting to become a doctor and work with Doctor Sydney Scott in her coroner's office and specifically in the morgue, *to* joining her parents who enjoyed success and a good work-life balance as private investigators. She would share this decision to work with them over coffee in a few hours. They would be surprised to see her and, ideally, both Paradise and Thomas would welcome her as the newest member of PIU (Private Investigators Unstructured).

Remembering the day she first met Clint and Jim, co-owners of PIU along with her mom and dad, Hope had to smile. She had thought they were interlopers crashing her parents' wedding celebration. When she observed both men sneaking out the exit door she raced after them, only to be mortified when they shared who they were and why they had come from out of province to the Cape for this special wedding. Hope quickly recovered, and her initial rather harsh attitude was forgiven. She hoped Clint and Jim remembered her version of events!

She missed her brother, Lee, although he would not be home when she arrived. Lee and his two super uncles, Uncle Denis and Uncle Waine, had finally convinced Paradise and Thomas to allow them to take Lee to visit Honolulu, Hawaii, his birthplace, for the summer and one full school term. They had worn Paradise down over time. Thomas had no objection to Lee's trip, given that he was born in Hawaii and his mother, Wikolia, was born and buried there.

Once the decision to move to Cape St Mary was made and before they boarded a plane the family of four had tried to find Lee's family, but after several days of searching they realized they were going around in circles. Lee was too young to understand, but they would explain their failed efforts once he was old enough to understand.

Not long after they had moved and settled, the uncles found them, much to everyone's delight!

The 'big guys' lived in cabin #3 at the Cape View Motel and Cottages. #3 had been known as a place to party, but once Lee began staying with them more and more often, the uncles put an end to the parties.

"That's no damn way to raise a young boy," said Waine, and who could argue with that? Not Denis; in fact, he was very proud of his brother, who had taken charge of making their cabin 'kid friendly'. Beer in the fridge was okay, but that was it.

Hope had shared the drive to the Cape and back to the city with her mother many times. In fact, Paradise was behind the wheel often. Hope knew that, with traffic, she would be on the road for at least five hours. She had already stopped once for coffee and a chocolate chip muffin, but would soon need to eat again. Sydney's chef had spoiled her and her mom with every meal. This included a nighttime snack left outside their door as the chef made her way out of the mansion to her own home.

6: What news trumps my news?

Paradise and Thomas had been awake for hours, talking in hushed tones about their guest, Penelope.

"I don't even have her full name, Thomas. I have been working exclusively on finding her for years, yet I am missing her middle name and her last name."

"Paradise, I have a feeling we will learn everything we need to know today. Conversely, we might learn nothing, because our young guest might leave us even before she has a coffee."

The conversation continued as they ventured downstairs.

At the bottom of the staircase, they observed one large suitcase, followed by a duffle bag, a backpack, an overflow briefcase, banker's boxes piled high, a purse and Hope. Hope in a deep sleep, half on and half off the sofa.

"Let's get the coffee on and then wake her up," Thomas whispered. "Normally I would suggest we let her sleep, but she needs to know about our guest now residing in her room. Preferably before Penelope appears. I can't wait to see them meet her, Paradise."

Thomas was off to the kitchen to light the stove. The house was freezing. Hope slept with her clothes on, so was instantly up and ready for that first cup of coffee. "I promise to cart all of my stuff up to my room but first I need to speak with you both."

In the kitchen, Hope kissed both of her parents and took her place at the table hoping her parents wouldn't be disappointed in her for giving up on her dream of being a Medical Examiner. Hope had come to realize this wasn't *her* dream at all.

She was surprised when her mother spoke. "Sweetheart, I can guess why you're home just by looking at the pile of things you brought with you. Did you leave any personal items at Sydney's, or are you totally out of there? I am especially interested in your last discussion with Sydney. I haven't heard from her so I'm guessing you asked her to stay quiet for a day or two. Long enough to give you time to fill us in yourself. Am I correct?"

Paradise was smiling and Hope took this as a good sign. She nodded, and sat quietly.

Thomas spoke up. "Hope, before you share your story with us, we need to fill you in about a development in our 'X' files case your mother has been dedicated to these past few years. Time is of the essence, as they say."

They sat in silence, enjoying that first cup of coffee. Other than Lee, when he was a pre-schooler, no one spoke while they were savouring their coffee.

After drinking the very last drop, Hope spoke up. "Mom, Dad, I've missed this!"

"I agree, Hope. Your dad and I have missed starting our days with you."

"Okay, then, speak up! What is your big news that trumps mine?"

Paradise dove in. "You may have heard bits and pieces about this file, but I will begin at the beginning anyway. This file is, or has been, confidential and labelled the 'X' files."

Hope interrupted, "I have heard you and Sydney talking about the 'X' files. Not enough to even know why you would be sharing it with Sydney, though."

"Remember to listen without interrupting."

"Sorry. Won't happen again." There wasn't much else Hope could say.

"Apology accepted. This very much involves Sydney. When she was fifteen years old, she was raped by a middle-aged man, a pillar of the community, friend to all and well-known to her parents. The bulk of the details are hers to share, but to understand where I entered the picture, you need this much: the rape impregnated Sydney. When she gave birth, she heard her baby cry. Only minutes later she was told her baby had died. Sydney never truly believed her baby was dead and to this day has been looking for her. She is paying me to find her. Hope, this may seem totally impossible, but late last night Sydney's daughter knocked on our door. Long story short, she is sleeping in your room. Her name is Penelope."

"Did I hear my name?"

Penelope walked down the stairs and sheepishly joined the family in the kitchen.

7: Even junk food

Standing in the kitchen doorway, Penelope was startled to see a young woman, possibly her own age, at the kitchen table. She had been expecting to see Thomas over coffee, and, of course, she already knew Paradise. She felt she had to speak up or bolt.

"Hello, Thomas." She extended her hand.

"Welcome to our home, young lady. Thank you for arriving on our doorstep last night. Seriously, I am so happy you made the trip. We all are."

"Enough with the small talk."

Turning to the stranger in the room, Penelope unloaded. "And you...let me guess. You're on Sydney Scott's staff and you came here to find out all you can about the long-lost baby birthed by a fifteen-year-old, the result of a rape. How did you find me here? How did you find me *so fast?*" Penelope was crying, wiping her tears and her snotty nose with the back of her hands and then hiding her hands in her pocket.

Paradise was about to speak when Hope gave her a sign to back off. Clearly, Hope was moved by the speech, if nothing else.

Thomas poured a cup of coffee for Penelope and then poured refills all around. "Penelope, how do you take your coffee? Do you need sugar, milk, cream?"

"I drink my coffee black, and it smells delicious."

Thomas couldn't resist offering one more comment. "Young lady, I see you take your mascara black as well." He slid a box of Kleenex across the table to Penelope, offering a tight smile.

Hope moved her chair so that she was right beside Penelope, extended her hand and said, "Hi, I'm Hope. Paradise and Thomas are my parents. I had no idea you were the child of a rapist. I do know that finding you has been my mother's singular job as a private investigator. She did not discuss your case with me, nor would she ever share such brutal information. I am learning your name *now*. Let's you and me take our coffee into the living room. There is a beautiful bay window facing the ocean. The window seats have padded cushions, and they are calling my name. Come with me."

Hope extended her hand. Penelope took it.

"Thank you, Hope. My God, I have made a mess of this morning. I'm so sorry."

Looking at her parents over her shoulder, Hope smiled. "Don't leave town, you two. We will be back."

Paradise whispered, "Thomas, we don't have enough groceries in the house."

Thomas nodded. "And we could use a bit of junk food, too, my love."

"Ladies, with two unexpected house guests we are going to make a fast trip to the grocery store, but we won't be long."

It was a short trip to the grocery store, and as they parked the car Paradise said, "Thomas, we are still crying. Let's take a minute to wipe our tears and find a couple pairs of sunglasses to hide our swollen eyes. How remarkable was what just happened back at the house? And did you know Penelope owned that trigger-temper that she turned on Hope?"

"I did not. I have met with her several times, as you know but always on her turf and always directed by her preferred line of questioning. It wasn't until she knocked on our door last night that I realized she had listened to every word I shared with her. From the day I met Penelope, I have had great respect for her."

With more than enough groceries packed into the car, Thomas and Paradise drove back to 548 Cape St Mary Road, and home. The first thing they observed when they entered their home was that all of Hope's luggage and even the banker's boxes had been moved.

They could hear the girls talking and realized they were upstairs in Hope's bedroom. They were also laughing a bit. This made Paradise cry all over again.

After walking to the bottom of the stairs and confirming that the mood had lightened a bit, Thomas shouted, "Ladies we have a ton of food and, Hope, your mother even allowed me to buy junk food. This is shaping up to be a great day!"

8: Trust

Hope and Penelope talked about 'trust.' They attempted to find ways to bond while sharing snippets about their own backgrounds. Baby steps amid high hopes. Trust issues threatened at every turn.

Hope wrote notes in her journal. After journalling for several minutes, she could feel yet another trust issue bubble to the top of the conversation. It wasn't the first and it wouldn't be the last.

"Why on earth do you want to commit our discussion to paper? I do not like this. What is this all about Hope? Honesty, please."

"*Really*? You *still* don't trust me? You've known me for one hour and you don't trust me. That is sad." Hope was smiling as she went on. "Penelope, I have already stressed that I would be honest with you, and I have been honest since we came upstairs. What can I do to make trusting me easier for you?"

"May I ask you to put your pen and paper down, please? I'm try-ing, Hope. Honest to God, I'm trying here."

"You win. Pen down. Seriously, Penelope, to recap, we have both spent many years separated from our birth mother. We are Type A personalities and overachievers. Example, you're a lawyer at the tender age of, what, thirty? Yet you're not sure you want to practice law."

"Ouch! I am not thirty years old. Twenty-five, and not a day older."

"Okay, good to know. I received my MD diploma at a young age, yet, instead of hanging out my shingle and getting on with my life I decided I wanted to be a Medical Examiner. Full disclosure, Penelope, last night I walked out on my personal tutor. You need to know my tutor was Doctor Sydney Scott. Notice I said she was, not is, my tutor. She's a workaholic and I have discovered that I want some work/life balance in my future. I put all my stuff in my car and drove home. I had been asleep for a couple of hours when dad and mom came downstairs and saw me. They were happy and they were shocked. I can promise you that when Sydney (mom and I call her Sydney, but Dad calls her Doctor Scott) learns you are here in the Cape and staying with us she will draw the conclusion that I quit and walked out on her so I could get home and learn all about you. You think you have trust issues? Wait until you meet your mother."

"I can't believe I am defending the good Doctor, but I wonder if she has reason to be less trusting since the brutality of her attack. Hope, is it true that my mother was raped and beaten almost to death? And, after a bit of digging, I heard that she had practically moved the morgue to her home so she could get back to doing autopsies. Do you know much about her personal life?"

Penelope paused and Hope jumped in. "My mother knows everything you need to know, so let's head downstairs and have a bite to eat. I do have one concern, Penelope. I will raise this with my parents and will do that in front of you. Sydney will be gutted to know that you have been in our home, and we didn't let her know immediately. Let's ask mom what we should do."

Scrambling down the stairs as if it was a competition, Penelope and Hope came to a halt as Paradise rounded the corner with the phone to her ear and said so they could hear, "I haven't even talked with your daughter or mine, Sydney, but I will. For now, I wanted you to know Penelope knocked on my door very late last night. We put her in Hope's bedroom, not knowing that Hope would be sleeping on the living room sofa when we came downstairs this morning. Thomas and I have been out this morning doing a gro-cery run. I believe the girls have been upstairs, chatting. Can you trust me enough to leave this with me for a few hours?"

"I do not trust you, Paradise, let me speak to my daughter. I need to speak with Penelope now." Sydney was yelling into the phone.

"No," replied Hope and Paradise in unison.

Paradise continued, "We will take our lead from Penelope, and when she wants it to happen...you *will* speak with your daughter.

Don't push her, Sydney. We don't want her to disappear, and I believe she will if we don't do this on her terms. Are you still there?"

"She hung up on you, didn't she, mom? Happens to me all the time."

Turning to Penelope, Hope said, "Let's enrol your mother in a Miss Manners course!"

"I might need the same course," offered Penelope. "When I first met my father, he was so rude and crude, even with me, to my face, while he was trying to 'win me over', as he put it, before the day came that I would meet my mother."

Looking first at Paradise and Thomas before returning her gaze to Hope, she continued, "Back then, I decided my father shaped me into what he wanted me to be...an untrusting and unfaithful member of my own family. Fearing everything he said about my mother was true, it was easy to believe him, for the most part."

Penelope ended it there for less than a second before continuing, "One thing I want to ensure we talk about, and the sooner the better, is that my father insisted my mother never told him who had raped her the night I was conceived. He made it sound as if she didn't know, because she had already been with so many boys at the age of 15! When he told me that, he couldn't look me in the face, and that gave me doubts about his stories...all of them. Please fill in some of the blanks for me, Paradise."

Paradise spoke in Penelope's defence. "You might have been rude in the first hour that you and I met, but I could see, even that quickly, that you very much want to belong to a family. To *your* family. Along came a stranger sharing the news that you did have a family waiting with open arms to meet you. A stranger who was being paid to find you, and money can come with mistrust, too. It was your own heart that brought you to us last night. You may have doubts, but they weren't strong enough to keep you away."

"Oh. My. God. Was that only last night?" Hope felt the mood should be a bit lighter and it worked. Paradise and Thomas start laughing and, sure enough, Penelope joined in. "My work here is done."

Hope disappeared, but not for long.

"Penelope, I would like to tell you a bit about your mother, but before I do, I need a nod from my mom just to be sure that she's okay with me doing this."

Seeing both of her parents nodding, Hope poured a glass of water for everyone as she gathered her thoughts.

Penelope said, "Can we call her Sydney, please? I am not ready to give her the title of my mother."

She spoke almost in a whisper, which prompted Hope to get up from her own chair and give her a hug.

"Hope, thank you for that hug. Until this very moment only one person in my entire life has hugged me. That was you, Paradise. You started all of this."

Penelope spread her arms wide, and without knowing it, she had invited everyone to hug her, and they did. A group hug. Another first for her.

9: I pay you to drive

Doctor Scott was haunted by flashbacks. And late last night they had returned.

She replaced the receiver on the wall-mounted phone in her hallway. This was the same hallway she crawled along the night she was raped and beaten nearly to death. Sydney visualized and felt the pain of standing on her broken and battered bones long enough to grab the receiver to the phone before she fell to the floor again.

Who do these flashbacks belong to and *why* are they haunting me?

> *What* happened to the confident me?
> *When* will this face look like me?
> *Where* is my shrink when I need him?
> *Why* can't I 'get a life', which is what no one says to my face, but everyone wants to?

Remembering her '5Ws', as she had labelled these questions so many months ago, Sydney decided she had better get out of her own way and do something different. A drive involving something of a personal nature, perhaps?

Doctor Gary Langille, Sydney's psychologist, had advised her to scream and yell at the top of her lungs if that helped her work out the kinks early in her day. He also suggested she needed to get out of her house. Even if she went for a drive and never got out of the car, that would do for now. "Just get out of your house. Use your own driver. I could drive you, Sydney, but that would not put you in the driver's seat, so to speak."

Sydney called her driver. "Chuck, pull out your map and pick me up in forty-five minutes."

"Doctor Scott, this is wonderful news. I haven't driven you anywhere in years. Not since—"

"The old me would remind you that I pay you to drive. To simply drive. However, as you have probably heard, I appear to have grown a personality, a conscience, and I have learned to not interrupt others...like I did with you just now. I'll fill you in when we head off to Cape St Mary. I believe it's about a four-hour drive. Just clear your schedule for the day. I realize you are due lots of vacation days, so start training your temporary replacement in the next little while. And, Chuck, I will refer to you by name going forward, with apologies that I just had to consult my computer to learn your name. God, I hope I didn't get your name wrong."

"Doctor Scott, you are never wrong. I appreciate you calling me by my name."

"Hold that thought, Chuck, I might be wrong about this decision of mine to go to the Cape. I will see you in forty-five minutes regardless of where we are going."

Sydney was indeed questioning her decision to barge in and introduce herself to her own daughter! But that was her exact plan as she jumped into the shower...for the second time that day.

10: The long way to the office

Driving the Medical Examiner once again brought a smile to Chuck's face. He had been idle for too long. While he delivered work to and from his boss, it was always to her residence, and always to someone else who would pass it on to Doctor Scott. In fact, they had not made eye contact in years.

Chuck had heard all the gory stories about her face and her body, and all the work that had taken place to put her back together again.

True to her word, exactly forty-five minutes after she had called him, Sydney opened her front door and made her way to a smiling Chuck, who was leaning against her car. He quickly stood straight and reached out to open her door, as he always did.

"Doctor Scott, welcome back. I, and many others, have missed you. It's been way too long."

"Slow down, cowboy, do not get ahead of yourself. Today means no more than me asking you to drive me to a specific location. To be honest, this trip is not work related and that's all you need to know. Do not ask…"

Chuck said, "Should I leave the city and head in the direction you asked me to plan out? Makes no difference to me, to be honest."

Chuck immediately knew he had overstepped with his 'makes no difference,' comment. He was right, she jumped on that immediately. That made him happy because in that moment she was the 'old' Sydney and he needed to know she was in there somewhere.

"Good to know, Chuck. I'm glad to know I am still in charge of making decisions. Let's drop the 'Doctor Scott'. Call me Sydney for today. In fact, whenever it's you and I, with no passengers, when we are out, I would prefer if you could call me Sydney. I'm trying to 'get a life', as Hope instructed me last evening before she headed to the Cape."

"Hope actually said that to you?"

"Does that surprise you? I think you know Hope, and have even driven her a time or two, correct?"

"I do know her a bit. I am shocked she would tell the Medical Examiner to 'get a life', though."

"You think you're shocked! I had to ask Hope to explain what the expression meant before I could comment on it."

"Sydney, this is fascinating stuff but am I driving to the Cape, or would you like a city of Halifax and area private tour?"

"Total change of plans. I think it's time you visit my offices," said Sydney. "That includes the morgue. It's not lost on me, young man, that you rarely enter the building and have never visited me in my office in the morgue."

"Now I'm worried. Just a minute or two you said this trip was not work related. Now you are insisting I visit the morgue. My boss would never talk in circles, so what have you done with Doctor Scott?" Chuck was smiling and Sydney played along.

"To the morgue, young man, to the morgue."

"You can show me every office, every closet, every security detail, and I know you have more than a few of those on site, but I am *not* going to visit your morgue. Deal?"

"Deal. Onward, young man. The morning is wasting away."

Thinking her last comment was very much the Doctor Scott he remembered, Chuck was relieved. But why, then, did her face, if it was her face, look like it belonged to someone else?

"Tell me, Chuck, has Hope ever shared her career goals with you? For several years now, she has been clear that she wanted to be a forensic pathologist. Yesterday she blurted out that she was quitting her university education because she wants to join her parents as 'private investigator-forensics.' She wants to be the forensics expert in the family."

Almost as if she was talking to herself, Sydney continued, "As you know, I had a morgue installed at the back end of my house. I took Hope to the morgue one day and, because I knew she had studied a specific textbook, I asked her to perform the proper way to take the temperature of the deceased to estimate time of death. She made the incision with the confidence of a seasoned pathologist, inserted the temperature gauge and gave the estimated time of death, again with total confidence. I took her to the morgue a second time, and, in her defence, she was not prepared for my demonstration of how someone had slit the throat of the corpse lying before us. Hope had to rush to the nearest washroom and ran from the morgue to her quarters, where she locked the door. I didn't see her until the next day. When I saw her, I did something I rarely do. I apologized."

Chuck felt ill just listening to Sydney. "Let me repeat, Doctor Scott. I am happy to have you give me a tour of your offices, excluding the morgue."

With a smile on her face, a smile that Chuck had not seen in many years, Sydney said, "You have my word on that, and I see our building just up ahead. In fact, it feels good just seeing it."

11: Rent-free

"Ben Champagne speaking. Who's calling?"

"Hello, Mr. Champagne."

"Mike, is that you? OMG, as Hope would say. Have you seen her?"

"Your young lady came home to the Cape in the middle of the night and, judging by the amount of groceries her parents purchased this morning, I would say she's home to stay. I think they know I'm staying in your cottage now, but I don't know them well enough to strike up a conversation."

"That's okay, buddy, I appreciate the call. As you know, I haven't spoken with Hope since her high school graduation, and that was at least six, maybe seven years ago. Her dad knew she bailed on me that day and he shared that her mom, Paradise, helped her pack her up and head to the city. She might be married with a few kids running around by now."

"Ben, remind me how long you were in the Cape after Hope moved to the city. I don't recall that you went back to France until a couple of years ago."

"You've lived in my home, rent free, since I left the Cape, so you can likely recall my departure date better than I!"

"True. I always panic when we talk because I have a feeling you're coming back here sooner rather than later. You'll give me notice, right?"

"If I decide one morning to jump on a plane, you can stay in the spare bedroom until you find a place."

'You don't have a spare bedroom!"

"Exactly. Enjoy my humble Cape castle while you have it all to yourself. And keep me posted on any Hope-sightings."

Mike heard his friend hang up before he had a chance to say

anything more. It was a game they played...who could hang up first. "We're not kids, Ben. *We're not kids.*"

Next on Mike's agenda was finding a place to stay when his landlord returned from Paris. He thought he might hang out at the 'Cape Boxing Club,' (CBC for short), just to see if Hope ventured outside. He could always ask her if she knew of any places for rent. Wouldn't Ben be surprised if he pulled that off.

To flush Hope out, Mike wrote a note to post on the bulletin board at the boxing club. He tried to imagine Hope reading his post.

> Looking for a small apartment to rent. ASAP.
> Currently renting Ben Champagne's cottage.
> All leads welcome.
> If the lights are on, knock on my door at #8.
> Call me at Ben's local number... 759 0808.
> PS Any and all help appreciated as I clean #8 to meet Ben's standards!

If Hope was interested at all, she would be in touch. Mike felt it was the least he could do since he hadn't paid Ben a cent and he had lived there just over three years! "Actually, I would love to meet and have time to talk with the young Hope," Mike said aloud, knowing there was no one within earshot.

The hour was late, but Mike knew the Boxing Club would still be open, so he decided to walk over and see what was going on in Mavillette on a weeknight. If lady luck was with him, he might be able to spar with another boxer who was at, or close to, his experience level in the ring.

It was Ben who gave Mike his start in boxing. Ben had helped some locals build the ring for Hope's younger brother. After lots of work over the months and years, the Club was finally turning a profit. They had purchased some land and built a bigger facility.

Mike was in awe of this small community. At a local pub some years earlier, Mike had struck up a conversation with Ben and was amazed at some of the stories Ben shared. Like how he met Hope at a wedding reception for her parents, Thomas, and Paradise. He hadn't been invited to the party but, according to anyone he spoke with, the entire community was invited. He would be forever grateful that he went.

12: Something big going on

Pops and Eugenie had missed Hope. They had not seen their granddaughter for months. She hardly ever came to the Cape.

They watched her run towards their front door, and were in tears as they opened it wide so they could step outside to hug her. A 'three-way' hug, they had called it when Hope was a small child. Tears all around.

"I'm sorry. I'm so sorry." Hope was the first to speak. She hadn't made time for either Pops or Eugene in so long she was afraid to put an exact length of time on it. "Do you know what's going on at my house?"

Pops couldn't let go of her hand. "When did you arrive home? We got up this morning and saw your car in the driveway, but it wasn't there when we went to bed. And we went to bed late last night, thanks to a great movie on the tele. It's called 'Erin Brock-ovich' and believe me, that movie makes you think about a whole lot of things that could be going in the wrong direction in this world. It came out in the early 90s, I think, but it's worth watching even at your age. It's not an old movie for old people."

"Hey there, Pops," Eugenie said, "give the girl a chance to speak. Hope, we couldn't believe our eyes when we saw you coming our way this morning. Oh, we have missed you so..."

She had to stop and wipe her eyes, but she had more to say. "Is it true that we have lost you to the city, sweetheart?" Eugenie had warned Pops not to ask the question and here she was, asking it herself. She gave Pops an, "I'm sorry my love," and continued. "Would you like some coffee, have you had breakfast, do your par-ents know you're here? Is there something going on at your house other than you coming home? We can't figure out how you could leave the Cape, my dear. I know I'm repeating myself, Hope, but we miss you so much. More than you could ever imagine."

"Yes, please. No, I have not. Yes, they do. Yes, indeed there is something big going on over at my house. While I have the floor—and, Pops, hurry up with that coffee—let me bring you up to date on my life. I have been at Dalhousie University, studying in the field of medicine...all things medicine. Both before and after being at university all day, I have been tutored by none other than Doctor Sydney Scott. Did Mom tell you that part? It's all true, trust me."

"Paradise has told us very little about your absence from the Cape or your university studies, so we don't ask. Or we try to not ask. Here's your coffee, black as you like it. Go on, Hope. We want to know everything."

Pops sat back down and, again, reached out to hold his grand-daughter's hand. He thought he might never let go.

"Best coffee ever. Thank you, Pops. Sydney is the most kind and caring individual that mom and I have ever met. We were assigned one wing of her estate. We have our own rooms and a third bed-room we use as a study. We have a full living room, equipped with all good tech things. We share a pantry with Sydney and we often have our supper with her. Mom has been in the city less and less. If she didn't keep you updated on my world, I'm guessing you don't know who Penelope is."

Hope stopped long enough to reach out and take a warm piece of a banana bread that had found its way to the table.

Eugenie said, "Oh, but we do know all about Penelope. All very hush-hush, of course, but we know your mother has been in and out of Halifax and in and out of Quebec, all to do with bringing Sydney's daughter home."

In her excitement, Hope interrupted Eugenie. "That's one of the reasons I'm here now. You won't believe this: just hours before I got home, Penelope knocked on our door. Mom wasn't expecting her. Thinking I wouldn't be coming home any time soon, they set Penelope up in my room." Pausing to get up and pour a refill for each of them, Hope sat down and hugged Pops sideways.

"I arrived home around 3 am, I believe, and honest to God, I could not even climb the stairs to my room, so I threw all my bags on the floor and within seconds I was sleeping on the sofa. I woke up when mom and dad came downstairs. Imagine their shock when they saw me, and imagine my shock an hour later when I saw a strange woman walking down the stairs from my bedroom! Penelope and I danced around each other, to be totally honest. My room seems, for a few days at least, to be Penelope's room, and I'm in Lee's room. When is he coming home from Hawaii, and will his uncles return with him? Both Lee and I owe our parents some quality time. I have never felt more sure of anything. I'll put 'call Lee' on my list of things to do asap."

"We know nothing about Lee, either, but we do know your parents miss him. Honey, how long are you staying, and will we see a bit more of you this time? We do miss you so much."

Pops still couldn't believe she was home and sitting in their kitchen just like she did before she was gobbled up by Doctor Scott. He didn't say that out loud. If truth be told, Pops was some mad at Doctor Scott for tearing his little family apart, even if it was only temporary. 'Temporary' can be a very long time when you're an old man.

"I don't have that answer for you today. I need to spend some time talking with mom and dad, and Penelope must talk with mom a lot more before she is ready to meet her own mother, so that's an immediate priority. I'm not sure how she feels at this moment. The harsh reality is that she can meet her mother any time so..." Hope left her thoughts on that for another time.

"My land, Hope, look out the window. Is that Penelope walking over with your parents? Pops, put a fresh pot of coffee on. Hope, clean the table and put all the dirty dishes in the sink. And don't dilly-dally, either of you. I'll cut more banana bread."

Eugenie was giving orders. In her kitchen, she was the boss. And there was nothing that she loved more than having her little family crowded around her kitchen table. She would thank the Lord for this blessing when she said her nightly prayers.

Pops opened the door wide as he had done when Hope arrived. "This is better than Christmas. Hi, Thomas, Paradise, and this young lady must be Penelope. Please come inside. There is always room around our kitchen table."

Hope gave her mother an inquisitive look, as if to say, 'How did you manage to convince Penelope to come here with you?'

"Penelope, come on in here and meet my Pops and his wife, Eugenie," Hope said. "Mom and Dad, I am glad to see you again too… and so soon! It seems like I just rolled out of bed, or off the sofa I guess would be more accurate and wandered over here for that all important first cup of coffee with these two. That wasn't a dig at you, Penelope, for taking over my bedroom. Just stating the facts folks. Just stating the facts." She was relieved to see Penelope smile as she moved further inside the kitchen.

Eugenie gave Penelope a warm hug and invited her to sit down with the family. "Thank you for stopping by. That means a lot to me. To Pops, too, I'm certain."

Penelope hesitated, then said, "Actually, I have a confession to make. Hope, I told your parents that I wanted to meet Pops and Eugenie, and then ask you if you could take me to your beach. I could use a long walk with a friend, if it's not too soon to call you my friend?"

"Girl, we are out of here."

Hope reached for her sweater and handed Penelope the sweater that Pops had only just hung up. "My people are the best. They will be totally okay with us eating and taking off."

"Do you think I could take a slice of this delicious smelling banana bread with me?"

Penelope didn't have to wait long for an answer from Eugenie. "Here, love, take a slice for yourself and one for Hope. Now skedaddle, the both of you."

13: Along Mavillette Beach

Hope and Penelope walked along Mavillette Beach during low tide, in silence. The sounds of the ocean were wrapped in the promise of a future they would love.

Hope broke the silence. "Penelope, we can talk while we walk, but sit here for a few minutes and listen to the roar of the ocean. The ocean speaks to me, but I have absolutely no clue what it's telling me. The smouldering waters will seduce you. Remember I said that! Does any of this make sense?"

"No," came the one-word answer that Hope expected.

Half an hour passed until Penelope spoke again. "Let's walk now, if you don't mind, Hope. I have a million questions and I don't have them in any particular order."

"Fire away."

"First question. Did you and Doctor Scott have a fight or something? I saw all the piles of clothing and tech equipment that you brought home, and I have heard your parents reference how long it's been since you were here."

"Fair question," Hope said. "I am the one who initially said I wanted to look after dead people (that's an inside joke your mom and I have). After your mom was beaten, she needed a ton of surgeries to put her back together again. That included re-attaching one of her eyes, if you can imagine. I was finishing up my high school education during the early days of her recovery. She moved her offices and a few of her staff to her home. It's a mansion, trust me. She needed years of physical therapy and, like anything else she had ever done in her life, she gave it everything she had. She has a shrink, of course. I haven't met him, but mom tells me he's gorgeous and doesn't take any bullshit from Sydney. I like both of those things about him. To answer your question, I kind of snapped last Friday evening. She was grilling me on things that might be on my next exam at Dalhousie University, that's in Halifax, and I was bone tired. I simply stood up, packed up my stuff and left the city. Sydney will see that I have moved out, and that will bother her. I will reach out to her soon. She deserves that and more. I think I'm burnt out at this stage, and that's on me. Sure, she pushed me to my limit, but I could have spoken up long ago and said, 'Sydney, enough!'"

"Hope, I know it was my father who tried to kill my mother. I only met him a few times, but he was full of 'let me tell you all about me' with never a question or any interest at all about me. I didn't like the way he talked about my mother, but he was all I had, or so I thought, so I tried to never anger him or make him not want to come and see me again."

"Dare I ask what he said about Sydney?"

"He told me that he did not rape her when she was fifteen. He said she 'came on to him.' I always wondered if she really did that at such a young age. He said that my mother did not want to see me or hear from me. He said he had an excellent standing in his community. Did tons of volunteer work. Went to church on Sunday with his loving family. In short, he always told me he was 100% good and Sydney was 100% evil. The last time I saw him, he told me he had a fool-proof plan to 'take her out' and that he had full cooperation from the Annapolis Valley police and from the warden in the prison they put him in. I nearly fainted when he said that! Does this shock you, Hope?"

"It does not. I didn't know some of what you have shared, but I will say I am really hoping you will agree to visit with your mom, even if you don't plan to stick around. Sydney told both my mom and me that while he was beating her, he kept taunting her with things about his wonderful life and about you and how close the two of you had become. The bastard made it sound like the two of you totally understand each other and that you have been best friends for some time. Sydney said these words were more painful than when he was kicking her in the face."

Looking at Penelope and how pale she had become, Hope knew she had to end this discussion for today. "I know you must have a million more questions, but let's move to discussions about today and tomorrow only, rather than yesterday. Would that work for you?"

Penelope wondered how she could have ever believed anything her father had told her. What a horrible man he must have been. One day she would look his family up, for no reason she could think of in the moment; but the thought had come to her while Hope was talking. She would develop the idea and then talk it out with Hope.

"Hope, I see a couple of people, and a tiny dog, coming towards us, and the woman is waving frantically. Do you know who they are?"

"I sure do. Wilmot is my mother's brother, and with him is his wife, Marie. Their dog never leaves their side. Theirs is a love story for the big screen, but I will save that for another day. I really want you to meet them. Okay with you? Oh, and their four-legged family member is called Rescuee."

Penelope was confused. "I can't imagine why anyone would want to meet me."

"Mom has been working exclusively with Sydney since the beating. Sydney has been razor focused on finding you and ensuring you are not in danger. Second, she is anxious to meet you." Hope realized she should stop talking…"I promise to let you ask some questions…eventually. Just one more thought: I think you should meet Sydney soon, because I believe every day that goes by with you staying here in the Cape with us, she will be sad, and possibly even hurt that you would come this far yet put off meeting your mother. Trust me: you will love her."

"Hope, would you drive me to Halifax and stay with me when I meet her? Maybe only for a few minutes, if my heart is racing as fast as it is right now as I simply consider meeting her."

"That might be the perfect plan, but let's run it by my mom. She is the one who 'found' you. I could see that this assignment was far more than work. It was personal, so she might want to be the one to introduce you to Sydney."

"Can we go back to your house now and talk with your mom if she has time? And what happened to that couple? I thought they were waving because they wanted to meet me?'

"I didn't wave back and that's our family signal on the beach. Because I didn't wave in return, they quickly understood we were having a private discussion and would catch up with them another time."

The ladies shared a laugh over the *family signal*, which was both simplistic and effective. Something to remember.

14: Is any of this ringing a bell?

Paradise and Thomas enjoyed their first cup of coffee while sitting outside on the back stoop. They had a few decisions to make and didn't want to wake the girls at such an early hour. Their track record for making good decisions while sitting on this stoop had not failed them to date.

"I should have replied instantly when Penelope asked if I would mind if Hope drove her to the city to meet her mother. She should go with whoever she is most comfortable with, and if that's Hope, I'm okay with that."

Thomas responded quickly "You hesitated because you want to protect Hope from the barrage of questions Sydney might hurl at her for walking out."

With a chuckle, Paradise said, "Well, there is that! I think Hope will likely excuse herself early in the discussion and retreat to what was once 'our place' within the mansion. I'm going to ask her to think long and hard about packing up her university books. Would that be 'for now' or 'forever?' I'm not sure she has thought this decision through, but at the same time I am thrilled she has come home."

"I am as well. Everyone in the Cape will soon be chatting about our girl. 'Is she home for good?' 'Has Hope finished her studies?' 'What's next for Hope?' It seems that folks here are more comfortable asking you and me rather than asking Hope directly, and I'm okay with that. You as well I suspect."

"Of course," replied Paradise. "One topic we have not yet brought up with Hope relates to her ideal job. She has enough university degrees to her credit already to enter pretty much any field she would like to work in. She must be certain she wants to join us as a Private Investigator not because it's the easiest job for her to 'apply' for, but truly the career she wants."

"Let's tread lightly with Hope, remembering she went from high school directly into Sydney's home and under her supervision twenty-four hours a day. I don't think she has had a break of even one day since." Thomas felt strongly about this, and he knew Paradise would take his comments personally. He wasn't wrong...

"Give me some credit, Thomas!"

He didn't think he had ever heard Paradise raise her voice to the point of almost yelling at him. This was a first. He remained quiet, knowing she had more to say.

"By the time our girl graduated from high school, you had been pretty much banned from Sydney's home. It wasn't personal, but, as she tried to heal both physically and mentally from the cruel beatings she took at the hand of Penelope's father, Sydney wasn't comfortable having any man enter her home. My God, is any of this ringing a bell?"

He could see her trying to settle herself.

"Are you thinking I'm to blame for Hope's desire to learn at the hands of Nova Scotia's chief medical examiner? And then she quit without any discussion with her parents...is that my fault as well? If you think for one second that I—"

Thomas stood and cut Paradise off as he raised his hands. "I'll get the coffee pot, and perhaps you could get a grip on your emotions. If the girls hear your tone, they will likely both want to get out of here. Penelope might think she is the cause of our words this morning. I don't even know you right now."

With that, he went inside to collect the coffee pot, and took a quick look in the girls' rooms upstairs. They were both sound asleep. Thank God.

Paradise was in tears, standing on the stoop, when Thomas returned. She silently held out the mugs. Setting the coffee pot aside, Thomas sat down with an angry look on his face. He wasn't sure he could continue this discussion, but he could see that Paradise was anxious to speak. He thought she looked nervous, but never had he seen her nervous. Not Paradise: she was the most confident businesswoman he knew.

"Thomas, my love, I am so sorry for my outburst. It seems that I'm suddenly overwhelmed with everything. First Penelope, next, Hope, maybe home for good. Finally, Sydney called wondering why I had missed our scheduled call yesterday. I told her Penelope was here and Sydney accused me of betraying her to enjoy Penelope in our home. I'm so sorry I snapped at you. I admit I feel better already, having unloaded everything that is in my head this morning. Not my finest hour."

With that Paradise sat down and took a sip of her nearly-cold coffee.

"Apology accepted. Before the girls join us, what do we tackle first?" He knew what Paradise would suggest.

"Penelope indicated that she would like to have Hope drive her to her mother, so that's what will happen. I'm hoping we can discuss this with the girls this morning and set a date for their trip. I owe Sydney a call. I think it's understandable that she is anxious, knowing Penelope is with us. What do you think, Thomas?"

"I'm sure this is what will be on the girls' minds this morning, so we can tackle that together and move it to our 'closed' column. I know that you need to have a few things crossed off your 'to do' list and this would be a good start. We will get through this together, Paradise. Have faith!"

15: The back stoop rule

Sydney felt blindsided and wondered if Paradise would have *ever* called her to talk about Penelope's sudden arrival. As it turned out, it was Sydney who made the call, only to find out Hope had arrived home safely with all her worldly possessions, including university books that Sydney had paid for. Additionally, Penelope, her daughter, was bonding with Paradise *et all*.

Sydney was fuming and knew this was not good for her health. She decided she would make the bloody call and then would contact her driver. She was determined to take charge of the situation. Chuck would be delighted when she advised him a trip to the Cape was finally happening, only one day later than planned.

As she reached for the phone, it rang!

"Paradise it's about time you called. Are you bringing my daughter here today, or do I have to come and get her?" Sydney knew how nasty her voice would sound to Paradise and she felt guilty about that, but she couldn't change anything now.

"Sorry to disappoint you, Sydney, but it's me, Hope. You sound a bit opinionated, my friend. You might want to lose that attitude before you meet Penelope. She and I talked all night, I swear to God. We haven't even run this past mom and dad yet; they're sitting outside on the back stoop. We have a rule in this house. If someone is sitting on the back stoop leave them alone. They are there because they want to be alone."

"Hope, why are you calling me?" Sydney knew Hope could talk in one long sentence and never actually arrive at the subject of the call. "I don't care about the damn stoop. I want to see my daughter. Talk about *that,* please."

"Yes, ma'am, you make a good point. Penelope has asked me to drive her in to meet you, and for us to stay overnight. I thought maybe I could make the introduction and then give the two of you some privacy by retreating to the wing of your home that doesn't belong to my mother and me any longer."

"That's a topic for another day, dear. I will anxiously await your arrival with my girl. She does want to meet me, I hope."

"She sure does, Sydney. *She sure does.*"

~

Hope made another pot of coffee and went to join her parents. She got right to the point. "Mom, Dad, I just called Sydney. I knew you wouldn't mind. As soon as Penelope showers and packs an overnight bag, we are off. Assuming they will have dinner together, we are going to stay overnight. I won't dine with them though. That should be private between the two of them. Not to say I won't ask questions when we settle in for the night, though!"

"That sounds perfect, sweetheart, but emotions will be running high and it's a long drive. Promise me you will drive safely and stop now and then for snack breaks." Even Thomas was emotional, and Hope and her mother weren't far behind.

Paradise stood up and stretched. "Hope, you go upstairs and make sure Penelope is ready to do this. Your dad and I will gather up some snacks and enough cold drinks to get you to the city and back. I do think staying overnight is a good idea." Paradise was talking to the back of Hope's head. She took the stairs two at a time.

"Paradise, I could prepare a nice breakfast for the girls. Sending them off with a full tummy is about all we can do for them today."

"Roger that," said Paradise with a playful smile. "Once the girls are on the road, I will call Sydney to let her know. I also want to re-spectfully make a suggestion that might be helpful as the day evolves."

"I totally agree. You are wise beyond your years. Our years are creeping up on us, don't you think?"

Paradise reached out to grab Thomas. "Speak for yourself, old man. You're a full three years older than me, and don't you forget it!"

16: Give me twenty seconds

"Guess who's coming to dinner? Doctor Gary Langille, that's who," he heard Sydney shout before he was out of his car.

Gary had fallen in love with Sydney some years ago, but had kept that to himself. He knew she had feelings for him but, it had never been the right time to introduce the topic. Gary was, after all, her doctor. Her psychologist. They had become friends...never anything more.

Nova Scotia's Chief Medical Examiner and the head of Psychology at the largest hospital in the province had been dancing around 'dating' for some time. Sydney had never been married, and she understood that Gary had been married too many times to count. An interesting mix for both...if a relationship should happen.

Early in their doctor/patient relationship Sydney had given Gary the moniker of' Shrink', although she was aware he did not appreciate the slang. She was trying to remove that from her vocabulary, but she still slipped now and then. Gary had let her get away with it.

The doctors met only days after Sydney had been raped and beaten in her own home. She had fired her first psychologist after one session, and Gary was determined to last longer than forty-eight hours. So far so good.

While Gary was on the tennis court early that morning Sydney had left an 'urgent message.' All Sydney's messages were urgent, but her latest message seemed more urgent than any of the numerous messages she had left.

"Gary, call me as soon as you can. I have the most exciting, frightening, and personal news this morning. You won't believe it. I can hardly believe it myself. Coffee is on and breakfast is available. I could use your advice before *my daughter* arrives. I could say that a million times...*my daughter*. Gary, you are going to see me, perhaps for the first time, with a smile plastered across my face. Please stay for dinner...it might be a very long day, and I might need to debrief with you after the girls are settled for the night."

Within the hour Gary pulled into the massive circular driveway surrounding Sydney's home. He wondered how her daughter would react to her first visual of her mother's 'home.' He also wondered how certain they could be that she was about to meet her actual daughter. He would keep that topic for another time.

The hour was still early as Sydney stood on her front porch with a smile on her face and her arms opened wide. 'What do I do with that?' thought Gary.

He got out of the car with both hands up and a warning. "Sydney, I just played a tennis game that lasted over an hour. I saw your message the minute I stepped out of the shower, and I have not yet had my first cup of coffee. In the name of everything holy, please fill a large mug of coffee for me."

Gary was smiling, and Sydney joined in. "Do not move a muscle. Give me twenty seconds."

Sure enough, she was coming through the front door in record time with a steaming mug of coffee.

"Thank you."

"You're welcome, now get in here. I need to talk with you before my daughter arrives." Sydney practically ran back inside, balancing her own coffee cup as she moved.

"When will that be, exactly?"

"They left for the first time an hour ago. Paradise called a second time to say the girls had stopped at one of the neighbours and she would call again when they left and hit the highway. And she did, about an hour ago. It's about a four-hour trip, I believe."

"Sydney, let's settle down and settle in, as we do at the beginning of every session. Before you remind me that this is a personal visit, I do know that. First and foremost, though, as your psychologist, I need to gauge your mental health. How are *you* feeling?"

Sydney wanted to interrupt but she held back because she knew her shrink had more to say. He didn't disappoint.

"Remember, Sydney, I don't know anything about your daughter. I didn't know her name until I received your message early this morning. I assume she was born when you were fifteen." Sydney nodded in agreement, so Gary continued.

"It might be difficult, but let's imagine how you will feel when your daughter and Hope step out of the car. I know you rarely, if ever, shed a tear around others, because you are so often unable to show emotion. I believe you will shed many tears before today turns into night. Try to be as comfortable with your emotions as possible. Not an easy task for you to complete, I know. Look to me for assurance, if that helps."

17: Road trip

Penelope had never been to Halifax. Hope would have liked to stay away from all-things-Doctor-Scott for a while longer, but she knew this was not about her. Packed and ready to go they pulled out of the driveway and on to Cape St Mary Road with the intent to leave the Cape in the rear-view mirror.

But just prior to turning left and away from the prying eyes of the Cape, Hope had an idea.

"We haven't had time to talk about *boys* yet, but I see a car in the yard here at #8. I'm going to stop and introduce you to a *hottie,* assuming my friend Ben is back from wherever he has been living these past half dozen years. Do you have a boyfriend, Penelope?"

For a second Penelope seemed startled. "No but I would like to have one. Are you going to introduce me to my future boyfriend right here? Just seconds from your parents' home?"

"Ben is technically already *my* boyfriend. He's also technically *not* my boyfriend, but I can fix that as long as he isn't married now, with a bunch of kids. If the dude living here is some other guy, he's all yours."

"I'm looking for a man above one you would call 'some other guy' so no matchmaking today please." Penelope was laughing and that made Hope happy given what their day would look like in a few hours.

"Well, thank you, Jesus," whispered Penelope as the door to #8 opened and a beautiful man stepped outside. "I'll have that one, please. Tell me that's not Ben."

"Good morning, ladies. Are you here about the note I placed on the bulletin board over at the Boxing Club? My name is Mike, and I rent this place. Interested in taking it off my hands?"

Mike looked past Hope and smiled at Penelope. "I won't bite. Do you ladies want to come in? Coffee's on, although I can't promise it will be up to your standards."

"We'll take a rain check. I'm Hope and my sidekick for the day is Penelope. Is Ben home? I'm looking for him. I saw lights last night, so…."

"Sorry, Ben's not here at the moment. Or at any moment recently. Sorry, again: I just got up and my brain's tousled."

Hope felt Penelope's presence right behind her and wasn't sure why she had gotten out of the car. "Mike, I'm Penelope and I'm *not* looking for Ben. Eventually I will be looking to rent a place, but I'm not sure it will be in the Cape. I might have a place in Halifax already. Without sharing details that would put you back to sleep, Hope is driving me to Halifax so I can meet my mother, for the very first time. And that's enough information for you, my beautifully-tousled new friend."

Leaving Mike with her best smile, Penelope returned to the car.

"Okay, Mike, that's enough about Penelope, who I have known for less than forty-eight hours, by the way, so I, too, just learned things about her."

She turned to look at Penelope, who gave her a shrug, suggesting she was more than *a bit* interested in meeting this man.

Both ladies were thinking the same thing: "We have so much to discuss en route to Halifax and back again later today". That would be assuming that 'later in the day' included both ladies. It would, more likely, be Hope flying solo at day's end if Sydney asked Penelope to stay with her. Hope gathered her thoughts and formulated her questions for Mike. "Where is Ben? Is he coming back to the Cape? If so, when? Do you have a contact number where I can reach him?"

"Come on in. I'll give you Ben's phone number. Even better…I will dial his number and hand you the phone. I know he's been crazy in love with you for as long as I have known him. Ben pays the phone bills, so the only long distance calls I make are to him. As soon as he answers, I will go out to the car and keep your friend company."

"Oh, I just bet you will keep Penelope company."

Hope was laughing as she took the phone from Mike. It was ringing.

"Champagne"

"D'Entremont"

"Hope?"

"Ben?"

"Hope, my beautiful girl, I have missed these one-word bantering discussions with you. What are you doing with Mike, in my cottage, using my phone? How in the name of God did Mike find you so quickly?"

"Where are you? I don't even know if you live here or have moved away. If you've moved away, I bet you have a wife and four kids by now, and you are dutifully following 'the wife,' away from our beautiful Cape and Mavillette Beach. How am I doing so far, Mr. Champagne?"

"Look at you, using more than a couple dozen words in the same response. Are you a Forensic Scientist already?"

"Nope."

"Medical Examiner?"

"Nope."

"Give me a clue."

"I must go. I am delivering a very important person to her mother and she's waiting in my car. Mike is talking with her. He's a good guy, I assume, because you're letting him stay here."

"Phone number, please."

"Mike has it. I will give him the phone and he can fill you in on how he tracked me down, assuming you wanted him to track me down."

"I did"

"Excellent."

"Hope?"

"Yes?"

"I have never stopped loving you."

His admission met the sound of silence. Jumping out of the cottage, while noting the front steps were missing, Hope was at the car within seconds. "Mike, I have left the phone line open. Ben wants to talk with you, and, Penelope, we do not want to be late arriving at your mother's place."

Hope started the car and the journey continued. "Who wants to share first?" Hope was totally okay with Penelope taking the lead.

Two young ladies with 'boys' on their mind...were taking a road trip!

18: Roses for throwing

Ben Champagne thought back some seven years ago. He had fallen in love with a young lady he saw across the room, in a silk dress fitting her every curve. They danced the last dance at Hope's parents' wedding. She had hosted the party and was busy all night, but when *Save the Last Dance for Me* roared through the speakers, Ben watched her glide across the dance floor to him. And they danced…

Hope was three years younger than Ben and a couple of years away from her senior prom. They agreed to give each other space. Ben would pick her up for her prom but, for reasons he still did not understand, Hope was not home when he arrived via limo, carrying a dozen red roses. Thinking she might want to leave the roses at home, Ben had the bouquet in hand as he rang the doorbell at 548 Cape St Mary Road.

"Ben, what are you doing here?" Thomas seemed confused.

"I know I don't have the wrong date. I am here to pick Hope up for her senior prom. Is she ready?"

Ben looked around Thomas and into the home for a glimpse of his date. He saw no one. Ben had waited a few years for this evening when they would, ideally, begin anew their boyfriend-girlfriend relationship. Slowly, very slowly.

"Ben, I'm sorry, but Hope is not getting ready. She isn't even home."

"How can that be? I don't understand." Ben was becoming agitated and threw the roses onto the nearest chair.

"Again, I'm sorry. I understood Hope and Paradise were heading to Halifax after a rushed call from Doctor Scott, but they were to stop at your cottage for Hope to apologize for cancelling one hour before prom."

"Was there an emergency with Doctor Scott?"

"I don't know. I just got home so I could see Hope in her prom dress and wave you two off."

"Man to man, what do you think is going on here, Thomas? I trust your opinion." Ben was totally confused.

"I think my daughter got cold feet about going to the prom with you tonight. Ben, please know I am grasping at straws here. I don't know what to think, and I give you my word: the minute I talk with Paradise I will call you. Regardless of the hour."

"No, let's put all of this on hold for now. I don't want Hope to run further and further away from me."

Years passed. Seven, to be exact.

~

That was then, and this is now, thought Ben. He had finally spoken with Hope, and that gave him optimism. He wouldn't buy that airline ticket back to Nova Scotia just yet, although he would fly with no luggage at all if Hope asked him to return to the Cape tonight.

19: She didn't just fall

Sydney paced through the ground level of her home...around and around she went. "I can't sit still, Gary. I'm walking better though, don't you think?"

"Yes, I have observed your walking technique as you round the corner and move from the living room to dining room, to kitchen to pantry, and back to me in the living room. I see a profound improvement in your hand-eye coordination and in your footwork as you round the corners in most of the rooms in this beautiful home. Seriously, well done, Sydney." Gary was trying to keep her mind off the arrival of her daughter. He knew it wasn't working, even for a second.

"For a minute there, I thought you were going to give me an, 'atta girl'. Am I right that when they called earlier, they advised an arrival time of fifteen minutes ago? What is wrong with young people today?"

"Knowing, and sticking to, the exact time is not going to impress your daughter. You have a driver who picks you up at home and drives you back home at day's end. You keep your head down and work until you've reached your destination. In fairness, I don't think you have the skill set to critique an arrival time to or from anywhere in this province within a fifteen-minute period. Especially for a couple of young ladies who have more than a four-hour drive to get to you. Sydney, to your knowledge, has Hope ever driven into the city without her mother in the car, and taking turns with her behind the steering wheel?" Gary hoped he hadn't overstepped.

"Ouch! Thanks for the smack upside the head. You have pointed out a few times where I could have easily let the small stuff go. I'm trying but, please, do keep calling me on it! Maybe not today though. My mind is otherwise occupied."

For a second Gary saw a smile on Sydney's lips. She rarely smiled, even though he had complimented her on her smile and suggested she might consider smiling more often. He made a mental note to ask her to share what used to make her smile, before that terrible night when a maniac broke into her home and tried to kill her.

Sydney walked back into the living room and he observed she had reapplied a bit of makeup. Nova Scotia's Chief Medical officer and Coroner was transitioning from her professional to her personal life before his eyes. She had become a mother!

"Gary, look at that car parked at the side of the road just before the entrance to my driveway. You've seen Hope's car. Is that her car and, if so, why is she parking there? Do you think we should walk down there and—?"

"*No, we are not walking down there.* I can't say that forcefully enough. The car does belong to Hope, but it is not parked. She has merely put her blinkers on and pulled over to the shoulder. Consider the possibility that your daughter is preparing to finally meet you and needs a minute to breathe. Hope, her driver, is the same young lady you have worked and studied with day after day, month after month. Two young women with very different thoughts in the moment. Are you sure you want me to stick around? Does Hope know you have asked me to be here?"

Gary stood and invited Sydney to check the driveway. The young lady sitting in the passenger seat of Hope's car was *her* daughter. "Open the door, put a smile on your face and think like a mother."

"Sure," came Sydney's one-word response, a habit Gary believed she had picked up from Hope. She was already wiping tears from her eyes.

Hope's car door opened first. Walking around to the passenger's side, she opened the door and leaned in to say something. A second young woman emerged holding tightly to Hope's hand.

"Oh my God, Hope, I'm going to either throw up or faint." Penelope was shaking and, as she fell to the driveway out of Hope's reach, a second set of arms was there to catch her.

"Did you hear her call me 'mother' as she was falling, Hope? Did she really call me 'mother'?"

"She didn't just fall, Sydney, she *fainted*. For God's sake, help her! You're the doctor here." Hope was pacing in circles around Penelope and Sydney.

"Here's a wet cloth and some water for your daughter, Sydney." Gary to the rescue. He gave Hope some water as well. "Let's get her inside."

"I'm okay now." Penelope's words were barely a whisper. "The water helped. Thank you, sir."

"Call me Gary, I'm a friend of your mother. You are about to meet and get to know one incredible woman. Just to be certain you have your strength back, please take my arm and walk slowly with me."

Lowering his voice, a fraction, so the others could still hear what he was saying Gary went on, "If you don't take my arm, your mother will pick you up and throw you over her shoulder. Don't make her do that, kid."

Sydney and Hope led the way, with eyes on Penelope to ensure she wasn't about to keel over again.

Gary gave Penelope's arm a squeeze and she squeezed back. This was going to be a good day. He could feel it in her arm and in the air.

20: Meet your mother

"Penelope," Hope said with a flourish, "it is my honour to introduce you to your mother, Doctor Sydney Scott PhD., Coroner and Chief Medical Examiner for Nova Scotia, teacher, friend, mentor and—her most important moniker of all—*your mother.*"

The girls had practised what Hope should say during their drive. As she began her introduction, she opened her arms wide and welcomed both mother and daughter to join her for a hug.

When she gently removed herself from the equation, the hug continued.

"Sydney, we did not practice the fainting spell. That was all your daughter. I had no part in it." Hope's plan was to lighten the moment, and it worked.

"Hope, thank you for that introduction," Sydney said. "Please, everyone sit down. We don't need to be formal; it all feels a bit stiff, I think."

Hope realized she had to keep the conversation going. "Sydney, Penelope and I talked about my exit to give you some privacy with your daughter, but feel free to kick me out if you want me gone now. In fairness to me, though, I think I should get to stay if *he* gets to stay." Hope was pointing at Doctor Langille and, again, she was successful in lightening the moment.

"You're good right where you are for now, Hope." Sydney moved to sit close to Penelope.

Gary said, "Sydney's right, Hope: for now, you and I should stay. When she does kick us out, I will take you for a meal. Are you both staying overnight or is that none of my business?"

"We talked about that during our drive," Hope said. "I know Penelope will be invited to stay but I'm not at all sure if I am welcome in what was *our* apartment. Mom and I stayed with you so often, but I'm not at all sure where I'm sleeping tonight."

Hope reached for her water and took a gulp giving herself time to decide what to say next. "I apologize for leaving under the darkness of night, Sydney. I owed you more than that."

"You owe me nothing, young lady. I was proud to be your teacher for so many years. I will say that some of the medical books you took with you have belonged to me during my entire medical career so, while I could replace them, I would much rather have my original copies returned. I'll remind you which books I am talking about before you leave."

Sydney took her daughter's hand as she continued, "In this moment, I don't give a rat's ass about books, yours or mine, Hope. I am just so happy you have brought Penelope to me. Regardless of the time, I have a full meal prepared, so let's eat. Take whatever you like off the sideboard and settle in. We can make small talk for a while longer and then I would like some alone time with Penelope."

"Sounds perfect, and I am beyond hungry," Doctor Langille said. and was out of his seat and first in line to fill his plate. "I do realize that I should have let the ladies go first, and it's only because I am on the doorstep of starvation that I have led the charge. I've left lots for you."

Looking skyward Gary added, "Bless me, Father, and forgive me, mother, and worry not, you did teach me better than my current actions would suggest."

"Sydney," Hope said, "assuming it is okay for me to stay overnight, I would like to make a quick call to my mom."

"You girls fill your plates, and let me call Paradise," Sydney said. "I need to step out for a minute anyway. Feel free to begin eating without me, as Gary has already done."

Not lost on Penelope or Hope, Sydney gave Gary a gentle pat on the back as she moved out of the room.

Hope was on her feet and playfully pushing Gary aside. "Get out of our way, please. This could be the last meal of the day that Penelope and I eat, so we will need seconds even before we hit the dessert table."

Looking at her friend, Hope added, "Earth to Penelope, are you eating or not?"

Penelope gave her head a shake as if to loosen the cobwebs in her head. "I am stunned to admit that I already think of this formidable woman as '*my mother*', so you'll pardon me for all of the emotions swirling around in my head."

She wiped her eyes and picked up her plate.

Never one to let an opportunity to help someone pass, Gary offered quietly. "Penelope, I don't know you at all, but I'm going to go out on a limb and say your emotions, while they are uniquely your own, are like those anyone in your situation might be feeling."

Counting on his fingers, he continued, "Nervousness, anxiety, fear, mistrust, disbelief, aloneness, interest, and both friendship and love are quite a load to bear. Your mother will be here to help you. And so will I, if you would like my help. All that is for another day and my plate is now empty so, chop chop, ladies: load your plates and sit down so I can go for seconds."

21: Afloat

Hope, afloat on an expanse of unresolved troubles, was certain she had no visible shore to swim towards. However, she resolved to keep swimming as long as her strength would allow.

"Hope, sweetheart," Paradise said over the phone. "How are things between Sydney and Penelope? Are they talking with each other? Is it awkward? Sydney called us for a few minutes just after you arrived, but she seemed awkward during our brief call."

"It's stiff, mom. I will admit that. They are, understandably, dancing around each other. I was happy to leave them to have dinner without me. I brought my dinner to our former quarters, and I am happy to report there are no signs that we have been evicted from this space."

"Now is not the time to worry about any of that. Are you okay, Hope? You sound a bit sad...am I reading you correctly?"

"You are. Penelope is just starting her life with Sydney, and I have ended mine with a solid crash against all the hopes and dreams Sydney had for me. That's on me. When I packed up and came home, I had planned to talk with you and dad about joining PIU as a forensics consultant or expert. I don't even know what I want to have on my business card, which is kind of funny. I don't know if you remember when I was a kid and wanted my own business card. I was worrying about what I should put on my card way back then."

Hope paused in thought.

"Hope, that was then, and this is now. When you come home, your dad and I will spend as much time with you as you need. Everything does *not* have to be solved immediately. You'll be the one to figure out 'next steps' but we will be right beside you."

"Thanks, mom." For a second, Hope could almost see the shore.

"Get some rest, Hope. Maybe we will see you tomorrow? If you end up staying in the city for a few days, walk around, visit the museum or the public library. I know that for all these years you have been under the direction of one Doctor Scott, neither she nor you saw the light of day once you arrived home from your classes. And Saturdays and Sundays were all-Sydney, all day and all night. Don't fall in love with Halifax, though. I need you to come home."

"No fear of that, mom. Although as you recapped for me, and seriously thanks for the reminder, I know nothing about Halifax, so I will be a tourist for a few days. I don't really want to drive back and forth too many times, to be honest, but if Penelope wants to get out of the city, I don't mind a couple of trips back and forth."

"I do have one more thing, daughter dear. Guess who called here, asking if he could have a number where you could be reached in Halifax? I'll give you a hint: you and Penelope met his tenant on your way to the city."

"No! Not Ben? OMG. Mom, I forgot to tell you we stopped in to see if he was around. You were right, though. He lives in Paris. I didn't realize he had kept the family home after his parents died." Hope didn't want her mother to think she had deliberately kept this news from her. She tried to remember everything that happened with that 'drop-in' visit.

"I heard all about your visit from Ben and, I will say, it was very nice speaking with him. I told him to drop in when he's back in town and he promised to do so. Is it okay that I gave him your number at the big mansion?"

"Yes, of course. He hasn't called, though."

"I told him a bit about Penelope and why you were in Halifax. I said the first twenty-four hours with Sydney might be heavy for you to be part of, so, Hope, blame me for suggesting he wait until tomorrow evening to call you. Have another dinner in your suite tomorrow."

"Mom, Penelope just walked in, and she is all smiles. I really want to talk with her. Catch you tomorrow. Love you."

Hope could tell that Penelope was tentative and possibly a bit confused. "You don't have to knock on my door, girl. Get in here. Give me a hug. On a scale of one to ten, how has your first visit with your mother been?"

"Ten. *Absolutely a ten.* I'm even calling her 'mom' and, as you know from our windshield time driving here, this was one of my big fears. Would she expect me to call her my mother, and would it seem strange to me. She applied no pressure at all, but she did acknowledge there have been some moments when we are both totally quiet. Mom suggested this will be our normal at least for a while. Since we are both living alone now, we do have opportunities to get away from each other. In fact, that's where we were in our discussions when mom got up and said, 'I have a full suite of rooms set up for you, my dear daughter, but for tonight I know you will be anxious to talk with Hope, so off you go,' and just like that she dismissed me after showing me where you are sleeping...nice digs, by the way."

Hope watched Penelope in all her excitement, but said nothing because Penelope was giving her some type of signal.

"Mom offered, and I agreed, that she will deliver our coffee in the morning along with some 'pantry stuff' as she called it. Is that okay with you?"

"Breakfast in bed. Delivered by the Chief Medical Examiner. Sure, I can live with that." Hope was laughing out loud at the mere thought of it.

Well into the night two young ladies who were becoming fast friends talked and laughed and talked some more. Additionally, they raided the pantry, not once but twice.

22: A difficult decision

Although he wanted desperately to move back to Cape St Mary in rural Nova Scotia, Ben wasn't yet ready to sell his family home in Paris. As he paced the floors of the house where he had grown up, he felt his parents' presence all around him. They left this earth wanting nothing but the best for their only child. 'Memories live in every nook and cranny.'

He packed up a few extra memories for this trip. He hoped to make new memories himself very soon. He would return to his cottage at 8 Cape St Mary Road. He would tell no one in advance of his arrival. Mark would be shocked to see Ben walk through the door. He knew Mark was seriously looking for his own place and he didn't even care if Mark was still living in his cottage when he arrived. He needed to walk on Mavillette Beach...with luck, holding Hope's hand. With a long-term plan in his head, he prepared to visit two charming ladies who lived next door. He had known them for years.

Knocking on his neighbour's door, Ben asked Rachel and her mother, Wanda, if they would keep an eye on his home while he was away. Wanda had once enjoyed gardening with his mother, and she had maintained the many mini-gardens his mother had planted on their grounds through the years. Ben was grateful to have such wonderful neighbours who loved his home as much as he did.

"Ben, we love caring for, and walking through, your gardens, and we love keeping a watchful eye on every room in your home. Your mother would expect no less," Wanda said. She was brought to tears easily, and always when she spoke of her neighbour and best friend.

Rachel was better at hiding her tears and fears. She stood beside her mother, always with tissues in hand to pass to her. "Here's a tissue, mother. Dry those eyes. Ben is going to stop coming over because his mere face turns your waterworks on."

To Ben she said, "So where to this time? Are you returning to Nova Scotia and the possibility of settling down close to the Atlantic Ocean? I'd love to bring mother to visit you one day, if you'll have us."

"Absolutely,' he replied. "Let me build a bigger home first, because my cottage is pretty much one room. Don't get me wrong. I love it, and if you could have seen #8 when I first visited after learning I owned it, you would better understand my pride. The folks living around me, now my friends, helped me rebuild #8 one plank and one roof shingle at a time. As I recall, at one point we had seven old buckets positioned in different places on my tattered floor to catch rainwater seeping through the holes in the roof."

"Surely you exaggerate, Ben!" Wanda said. "You seem to love the place, but it sounds so different from the home you grew up in."

"Cape St Mary has shown me that I can live in one room and be as happy as I am right next door to you in Paris," Ben said. "In fact, I have an idea that might benefit the three of us. I need someone to take care of my home and property here. Wanda, I know my mother would have been the same age as you. Given your disabilities I think my parents would want me to try to help you, if you will let me. Rachel, I know you are working part-time because you want to be with your mother so you can make her life a bit easier by being at home with her. Sorry I'm making this so long. I'll get to the point. How would you like to give up your apartment and move into my home? You know how huge the place is. I've been giving this a lot of thought. You could live on the main floor to avoid stairs, and when I return, I can very easily live on the second floor especially since we are friends already, and I promise to put clothes on before venturing downstairs to the kitchen. I hope I'm not offending either of you. Initial thoughts, please."

Rachel spoke first as she handed her mother yet another tissue, since she was really bawling this time. "I'll speak for both of us, mother, assuming that's okay with you."

After some thought, Wanda nodded. "Ben, you know us well. We could use some help, and to your plan of giving up our tiny apartment to live in your huge estate, I don't see any answer other than, yes, we would absolutely love to do this. But only if you're sure—"

"Sure. I am sure. I know you have lots of furniture here in your apartment. I will have the first floor cleaned out for you before I even book a plane ticket."

Wanda found her voice. "Ben. Ben. Ben. Your mother and I always used to say we believed that all men are colour blind. Do you think we would own any of this furniture, when no two things match in any way, especially in colour? There are no antiques here, just very old and run-down furniture that was here when we rented this place. We arrived with nothing but the clothes on our back. That's a story for another time.

"Your mother came over on our first day," Wanda said, "and her knock on the door nearly frightened us both to death. We made sure no one knew where we had relocated to, and yet someone kept knocking on our door. Mom looked over at me, nodding towards the door and I swear I stood there with both hands on the doorknob and said a prayer as I quietly asked, 'Who is it?' Sure enough, it was your mother, Ben. She brought us so many gifts, including a home-cooked meal, groceries to get us through a couple of days, and a map that included both bus and subway routes and schedules. She offered to drive us anywhere we needed to go until we had time to get our bearings."

Wanda smiled and continued the description to give Rachel a break. "We laughed after your mother left for a couple of reasons, mainly that she felt the food she brought would last a couple of days, but we knew that we could stretch it out for one full week. We studied those maps and routes until we had them memorized so by the time we ventured outside we knew exactly where we were going.

"Ben, things have changed for mom and me. Sure, we are still poor and we always will be. We have come to be okay with that. I'm not sure I'm saying this properly, or if that even matters. With a bit of caution, what I will say is that the fear we lived with before coming here, and the person who abused both of us, are dead. We are running no more."

Turning to her mother, Rachel continued, "Mom, let's not overthink this. Let's start packing as soon as Ben goes home, so when he tells us he has picked a date to fly to Cape St Mary we will be ready to move in."

Ben looked at Rachel. Rachel looked at her mother and her mother looked at Ben. "Son, we have some packing to do, so if you don't mind getting out of here, we would be ever so grateful."

"I have a flight to book, so let me take you both out for breakfast tomorrow morning and we can talk specifics."

Mother and daughter said in unison, "Okay by me."

Ben was off with a million thoughts running through his head. "She could be my lucky star. Hope, *you* are my lucky star."

23: A meeting of partners

"There was just the one item of business, right?" the voice said over the speaker phone.

Thomas and Paradise had set up a conference call with Clint and Jim Taylor, the other two partners in PIU (Private Investigators Unstructured), who lived in Port Credit, Ontario. Despite the crackly phone line, Jim's voice came through pretty well.

"Yes," Thomas said. "Just having Hope join the team."

"We haven't had a forensics person before, but I certainly can see how it would be useful," Clint said. "I don't always trust the official reports we get from crime labs, not least because I can barely understand them."

"Perhaps you two can work out a proposed contract with Hope," Jim said, "and after we pass it by our legal people, all that would remain is getting it signed."

"Roger that," Thomas said. "Paradise and I appreciate your interest in, and acceptance of, our daughter."

"She is a ball of energy," Clint said. "She may give us old folks a bit of a long-needed shaking-up."

After the call, Paradise got a fresh cup of coffee and sat down to re-read the very long letter she and Thomas had received from Hope. They had discussed whether they should share it with their partners, but decided that would be Hope's decision to make.

As she straightened the pages of note paper into a neat stack, she wondered how they had missed signs of Hope's struggles in Halifax. If they had spotted them, would they have stepped in to rescue her?

Hey Mom and Dad,

As you know, I have a desire to work in forensics. The first step is to get the right education. Forensic scientists typically have a four-year bachelor's degree in science or forensic science. I have a bachelor's degree in science, plus my MD degree. There are many post-secondary schools that offer forensic science degrees. Sydney gave me mine. However, as you know, I quit before she felt I was done. I will always be taking courses, and I might even return to university one day, but that's in the future. I won't rule out going to Sydney for a specific course just to get her opinion now and then, but none of that will happen until I do some practical work.

In a forensic science program, you take courses that will directly help you in your career, such as crime scene investigation, bloodstain pattern analysis, toxicology, and forensic DNA typing. Or if you already have a Bachelor of Science degree, like me, you can specialize in toxicology, pharmacology, biology, etc.

Sydney reminded me, more than once, that advanced specializations (e.g. forensic limnology?) require further education or more experience in the field. I'm not sure I had ever heard anyone use the word limnology, but it was easy for Sydney because she has more education than God... Sorry mom.

Paradise imagined Hope smiling as she wrote the reference to God.

You will love it mom: 'Limnology is the study of inland waters—lakes (both freshwater and saline), reservoirs, rivers, streams, wetlands, and groundwater—as ecological systems interacting with their drainage basins and the atmosphere.'

Mom and Dad, you may be pleased to know that limnology is of no interest to me. Not in my wheelhouse!

Paradise could see that Hope tried her best to paint a good picture regarding Sydney's desire to teach her everything as quickly as possible, even if Hope wasn't interested in certain medical departments.

> Sydney had this idea that I would become an expert in these areas if my goal should shift to forensics.
>
> - Toxicology
> - Forensic pathology
> - DNA analysis
> - Crime scene tech
> - Forensic biology
>
> She understands that, for now, I want to focus on forensic pathology. One of five…not five of five, all at the same time.

Paradise knew part of Hope's need to share this level of detail with her parents was to ensure they realized how much she took on at Sydney's suggestion. *More likely at Sydney's insistence,* thought Paradise.

> When I first began to study with Sydney, I said I wanted her job one day. Big mistake on my part.
>
> She immediately had me start studying everything relating to the Chief Coroner's job. During my last day with her she was quizzing me as if this were my final exam in my whole damn life. I got angry but I did rein myself in. You would have been proud of me.
>
> First up, I was to detail the responsibilities of a Medical Examiner and I tried my best. 'The Medical Examiner Service is responsible for determining the cause and manner of death in circumstances that are defined in the Fatality Investigations Act, but broadly include all deaths that are violent, unexpected or unexplained. The cause of death is the underlying disease or injury responsible for death. The

manner reflects the circumstances surrounding the death. If the death is due only to natural disease, then the manner is natural. If injury contributes in any way, then the death is not natural. The group of deaths that are not natural are divided into homicide, suicide, and accidental. If there is insufficient information available, the manner of death may be ruled undetermined.'

Sydney immediately turned on me. "That's it? Are you sure there isn't more to the ME responsibilities? Hope, you have been studying this for years, for Christ's sake. Where is your brain?"

My reply was quick. 'Sydney, I remembered, but you were so quick to berate me I couldn't get it in. ME service is also responsible for approving cremations, and I can't explain how that slipped my mind. What a tragedy. I'm sorry, Doctor Sydney Scott, I can't continue at this pace. I am going to move home. I have been neglecting my family. Honestly, I don't know how you do it. You are in business mode all the time. It's making me question my future, if this is what's required. Your number of working hours is insane.'

Sydney seemed stunned, as if she had never heard me complain before about the un-Godly pace she keeps with her work hat on. One night, well, it was past 2 am, so technically it was morning. I was still at my desk with Sydney looming over me. I asked her if we could close the books and go to bed, or at least talk about something personal, like when would she be comfortable leaving the house and returning to her offices.

Mom (and Dad too...sorry Dad I don't mean to leave you out), I will never forget how she answered. "Good Lord Hope, in your entire life have you ever seen a certificate on anyone's wall announcing a degree in personal life?"

I found this response profoundly sad.

I know this is one very long letter, but it's also a reminder for me. To become a forensic scientist in Canada, I have learned that I should consider three options.

1. Join local law enforcement, like maybe PIU.
2. Take a degree that allows me to work in forensics while I study.
3. Enrol at the Canadian Police College.

I pick door number one! Are you surprised?

All I must do before we begin figuring out if this is even possible is to prepare Penelope to stay alone with her mother. I don't want Sydney to overwhelm her as she has so often done with me.

I have Penelope's permission to move in with her! She will be in what was 'our suite of rooms', mother, and I can be in my old room.

I love you both...so much.

Hope d'Entremont

PS My dream title with PIU would be 'forensic investigator', if the four of you want me. Sydney has hinted that she will call on me to assist with forensic autopsies in her morgue as well.

24: Homesick

Many years had passed since Lee kissed his sister, his mom and his dad 'goodbye' and set out on the greatest adventure of his young life. His uncles, Denis and Waine, pleaded with Thomas and Paradise to allow them to take their nephew to his homeland, and at long last they had agreed.

Honolulu, Hawaii is Lee's birthplace and, sadly, it's also where his mother, Wikolia, was buried only a few years following his birth. His birth mother suffered from mental illness and, now as a very young teenager, Lee is already committed to becoming a doctor to explore mental health issues. In particular, he wants to study depression and how a patient is to cope when there is no specialist available.

One evening, when all three were at home, Lee made his pitch.

"Uncle Waine, Uncle Denis, was I supposed to stay this long when we first left Cape St Mary and boarded that huge plane that brought us here to Hawaii? You know I have this memory of my mom whispering into my ear that she would see me in a couple of months…three at the absolute most. Am I wrong about that memory? I've been wanting to bring this up for a year now. It's always on my mind. Did my mother and father give me to you, or are you keeping me from them? Don't be mad. You have been so good to me. You have taught me so much, plus you enrolled me in a private school that I absolutely love. And when I finish high school and begin my studies at university, I can earn money boxing and refereeing, all thanks to the two of you. I would like to visit a couple of universities in Canada, and more specifically in Nova Scotia."

Lee stopped talking to see if either of his uncles would speak up.

Dead silence followed.

"Shit, have I gone too far?" Lee had practised what he wanted to say, but it seemed he had put his uncles in a trance or something.

Denis finally spoke. "Lee, have you grown up while we weren't looking? It sounds like this conversation is well overdue."

Next, it was Waine's turn. "I wish you would have brought all your questions to us earlier. We thought we were keeping everything on the kitchen table for discussion over our big-breakfast mornings. I will admit that when you didn't bring it up, we didn't either. To put your mind at ease, Denis and I will take you home to your family anytime you want. If you don't want us tagging along, we are okay sending you on your own. We have been keeping your mother and father up to date, especially regarding your schoolwork. You could go home for the summer and, during that time, you might consider finishing your last two years of school here and then heading off to University in Nova Scotia, if that's what you want to do."

When Denis didn't add anything, Waine continued, "It's about you, Lee. It's always been about you, ever since we learned that your mother had died and that we had a nephew."

Denis said, "Me and Waine didn't even finish high school. Did you know that?"

"I did not know that. Given how well you both know your way around a private school, I would have guessed you graduated high school with honours."

There was one thing Lee wanted to thank them for, and now was a good time. "I know you wrote the school boxing program and made the school board approve it before I entered school. I also know you asked only that your wages for your work with the school be applied against my tuition and other costs. And I know that this past term, when you wrote the introductory boxing program for the junior classes, the school board cleared all my debts, including tuition for my next two years, if I choose to finish high school here. You might say you didn't finish school, but you are giants in the eyes of the movers and shakers who tie themselves to this private school by making such selfless donations to the school."

"By God," began Denis as he looked into his brother's eyes, "Waine, I think we just got ourselves a Grade twelve diploma!"

"Here's a promise I will make." Lee was on his feet. "I've just decided, right this second, I will return to take my last two years of high school here, and we three will walk across that stage together to receive our high school diplomas."

"You can't return before you leave, so let me check the airline flights. We will put a trip to Cape St Mary together for you." Denis was good at stuff like putting trips together.

"Hey, brother," said Waine, "I wonder what the chances are that Cabin #3 at the Cape View Motel and Cottages might be available for the next few months? Let's give Russ a call."Lee's emotions were on his sleeve, where he always wore them. "Oh God, I love that idea. I remember the sleepovers I had with you both in cabin #3. You made me feel like 'one of the boys', and you included me in everything. If we were going grocery shopping, you wanted to know my opinion on certain foods and if I couldn't read the label you would read it to me, and God help me if I lost my concentration and looked away. Do you remember?"

"Funny that you can carry all those memories with you Lee," Waine said. "You were so young you seemed a bit scattered at times. First, we couldn't get your attention, then we couldn't keep it." He was laughing and enjoying every second of the discussion.

"I remember the day we were driving back to #3 and you shared that there was a gift for me in our cabin, on my bed. You brought it all the way from Hawaii, and you didn't even know me then." Lee was enjoying this banter very much.

"Ah yes, the red boxing gloves," said Denis. "You were in love with those gloves, and they slept on the second pillow in your bed. Some mornings we would find you, sound asleep, wearing your pyjama bottoms and your boxing gloves."

"And the morning I wore those red gloves to the breakfast table and dropped my glass of milk because it slipped through my gloved hands. I had never seen either of you upset before. Waine, you handed me the dish cloth to clean up my mess and, Denis, you took my prized boxing gloves away from me. I never wore them to breakfast, or to any meal after that. And I begged you not to tell my mother."

Wayne could hardly stop laughing. "We promised to not tell your mother, and what did you do the very second we walked into your home?"

Denis said,. "You started telling what had happened before we were all the way through the door."

"I remember I said something like, 'Mom, I spilled all my milk and my uncles kind of whooped me.' Then I started fake-crying, but mom wasn't having any part of it. She said, 'Lee, you cannot sleep over at your uncles' until you have learned a bit about manners at the table.' And I said, 'I do know about manners at the table. I had already washed my hands for breakfast, but I had them inside my gloves. They were clean but my uncles just couldn't see how clean they were.'"

25: Shaking things up

By the look on their faces, both Hope and Penelope had been awake most of the night.

"Time to wake up!" Sydney said. "Breakfast personally delivered to your suite, ladies."

Turning every light on with the flip of a switch, she watched two bleary-eyed women jump up in bed, rub their eyes and try to focus on the source of this loud announcement. Penelope looked shocked. Hope fell out of her bed trying to see who was shouting at the top of their lungs. Sydney hadn't thought she was shouting at all.

Realizing it was none other than the Good Doctor, she couldn't stop laughing. "For the love of God, what time is it? It has to be about 5 am, right?"

"You wish," said Sydney with a smile. "I'm going to pour three cups of very strong coffee because, when I tell you what time it is, you are going to really need a coffee. Your day is half over. At exactly what time did you turn out the lights last night?"

"Mother, no games please," Penelope said. "Could you please hand me my coffee. I don't think my legs are awake. It feels like we have slept for nothing more than a few hours, so I'm guessing it is not even 6 am. Am I right?"

"It is damn near 12 noon, I swear to God."

Instantly, the girls were out of bed. Hope thanked Sydney for her coffee and Penelope was trying, without much success, to not spill any of hers. So far it was on her t-shirt and pyjama pants but not yet on the bed sheets.

"Sydney, in all the years I studied with you as my primary teacher, I never once heard you 'chuckle', and if you're going to tell me that 'chuckle' is not a proper word, I just made it one!" Hope held out her empty cup. "More of that yummy coffee, please."

Cup refreshed, Hope turned to her new friend. "Penelope, you haven't had much to say for yourself this morning. I'm going to grab a shower, so this is me slinking away. Don't eat all the food because I won't be five minutes tops. Oh, forgive me but I'm expecting a long-distance call from Ben in about twenty minutes, so can I ask you ladies to take your party elsewhere?"

Watching Hope move into the bathroom, Penelope said, "Mom, I'm sorry to say I bet it was after 4 am when we turned off the lights. And that makes this gift of a personally-served breakfast plus snacks even more appreciated. Let's move into your place so Hope can have some privacy for her call."

"Thank you, my dear daughter. You are such a grateful and humble young woman. I will spend the rest of my life helping you as you navigate your 'next steps.' Any thought as to whether you will stay here with me indefinitely?" Beneath the table Sydney had her fingers crossed. She knew she was moving too fast, but her thoughts spilled out of her mouth before she could remember to not rush Penelope.

"Hope and I have been talking about all the education you have helped her with. I 'm only a few credits away from finishing my degree, and would like to finish that off with a couple of courses at a university here in the city, and I sure could benefit from your advice. Education is very important to me but I had to stop attending classes and get a job to support myself. It's been an isolated life and I need that to change."

Penelope paused for a sip of water and seemed to be gathering her courage. "Mom, I think it's best if I use the bit of money I have saved and get my own place. Don't take that the wrong way, please. I've been on my own for a lifetime and, while I'm sure I will want to see you every day until I get settled, and maybe longer, at my age I think I need to have my own space. Do you understand?"

"Of course I understand. I'm not so old that I can't recall what I was like as a young woman. How about a compromise: at least think about it. Stay with me, I promise to leave you alone more than I do now, until we check into how best you can finish your degree. I can guide you through the process and I promise to not smother you as I did with Hope. I didn't even realize I was doing it! As you girls say, 'I need a life,' and Gary is helping me understand why and how I have managed to shut down and never leave this house."

Penelope crossed the room and hugged her mother for a very long time. "Mom, Hope has told me what you have been through. My father almost killed me, too, but in a different way. He kept visiting me with what seemed to be the sole purpose of filling my head with lies about you. Terrible things. He said you never thought about me. Then I met Paradise. Took me a bit of time to believe the turn of events in my tiny world."

Sydney returned the hug. "Now that I know you are interested in talking about all of this, let's stop for today. I have an idea, Penelope. Do you drive? I mean, do you have a driver's license?"

26: Making plans

"Champagne."

"d'Entremont."

"When did you start using your mother's maiden name, my love?" Ben said. "Are your mom and dad okay with that?"

"Is that a third-degree I hear being thrown at me through these long-distance telephone wires? Really, Ben?"

Hope enjoyed every second of their telephone banter. Every day since they had reconnected not quite two weeks earlier, Ben had called her, sometimes more than once a day. "Not to rush things, but when are you coming home?" She had only just begun to find her balance and no longer felt afloat without direction...at least not where Ben was concerned.

"I'm going to book my airline ticket soon. My neighbours, an elderly woman and her daughter, who were best friends with my mother, don't have much money to live on, so we have moved them into my home. You will see how huge it is when you come to Paris, my love. They will live on the first floor, and we will live on the top floor when we are here. I know you will love them."

"You are kind and charitable, Ben. I admire that so much. Can we talk business for a second." Hope was very proud of her boyfriend, but she had news, too, and wasn't sure how long they would talk at this earlyish hour.

"Fire away! What's on your mind Miss Private Investigator? But can we talk more about this gun issue when we are in the same room?"

"When I go home, mom is taking me to the shooting range not far from where we live. I've never shot a gun before, and mom says she hopes I never find myself needing to shoot someone, but she wants me to be ready if I am ever in danger on the job. I wonder if my parents will give me my own gun. I assume I will need a holster like mom and dad wear. Ben, if this all happens, don't you think it would be so cool to be on the PIU team?"

"Please keep this conversation until we are in the same room. Can you do that, Hope?"

She could hear the stress in his voice. "Sure."

"When you go back to the Cape, how long will you stay? Maybe you will still be there when I arrive. If you see my buddy, Mike, don't mention my return. I know he will stress about finding his own place, so when I surprise him, I will make sure he knows he can take as much time as he needs to find his own bachelor pad. Hope, when Mike called me after he met you and Penelope, he had a lot to say. I'm having fun with him because he doesn't even know her last name or anything about her, yet he's convinced he's already in love with her. Cute, eh?"

"How quickly you forget, Benjamin Champagne. I believe you told me you loved me when we had only just met and were dancing to my parents' favourite song, *Save the Last Dance for Me*. Does that jar your memory?"

"You forget I had hours to stand back and watch you move seamlessly around the dance floor in your slinky red dress. With a clipboard on your hip, you were clearly in charge. You and I did lock eyes once, which *gave me hope* that I wouldn't have to hunt for you during the last dance. When the song began, and you started walking towards me, in a very seductive way, I might add, I knew I was falling in love."

"Lovely words. Was the use of the pun necessary...*gave me hope*...? Really, Ben?"

"Perfect example of why we should not have such personal discussions over the phone. I didn't invoke any pun in my declaration of my love for you. I was, and am, 100% serious, Hope. I have been in love with you since that first night we danced together. Am I making myself perfectly clear, young lady?"

"Yes."

"Okay."

"Okay."

"This single word banter is cute, Hope, but it's also a bit childish especially when I'm wearing my heart on my sleeve. You're killing me here, my love."

"I'm hanging up."

Ben tried calling her back, but she wasn't answering the phone. He might not be staying in Cape St Mary after all. If there was no 'Hope,' life in the Cape would be both awkward and heartbreaking.

27: Call home

Lee called home, needing to hear his mother's voice. Wayne and Denis were his uncles, his boxing teachers and his friends. They became his temporary parents when he first moved to Hawaii as a young boy. Years have passed. He hasn't spoken with his mother. Not one time. Even his father has not been in touch.

He still called Cape St Mary his home. It's the first place he could remember living in.

As the phone rang, Lee found himself becoming emotional.

"Hello," came after just one ring.

Lee needed a minute before he could speak.

"Hello, is anyone there? Hello? Do I hear someone crying? I can help you. Please tell me your name."

Lee felt foolish and dried his tears. "Hi, mom, it's me, Lee. It's wonderful to hear your voice. How are you?"

"Lee, we can talk about me another time. Where are you, sweetheart? Are you okay?"

"I'm with Denis and Waine in Honolulu. Everything is okay, mom. We were just discussing that I have only two years left of high school. I would like to check out a few universities in Nova Scotia. If that's okay with you and dad."

"Lee, you never need to ask permission to enter our home and the *'our'* in our home includes you. Anytime!"

"God, mom, don't misunderstand. I was trying to be polite by asking if coming home would be okay. Waine and Denis have been nothing but parental and cool. They have played a huge role in my schoolwork, they taught me to ride a bike and how to box. Boxing is such a huge thing for us, however I am going to park this item, so you can have a turn at the podium. Do you still say, maybe to my sister, 'Hope, I am going to park this discussion for now, but we will come back to it'?" Lee felt a bit stronger after he heard his mother laugh.

"Mom, I would like to come home for a long visit *now*. I'm off school for four months and, while I'm not saying I would like to come home for that long because there is prep work required for my next term, I would be able to stay for a few months. Is my room still there? I know I've been gone for a very long time."

"My son, your room will be available for as long as you live. Do you have time to say hello to your dad?"

"Do I have to?" Lee knew his joke fell flat. "Joke mom, I would never hang up without hearing my dad's soothing voice. Is he home?"

"Not only is he home, but he is also wrestling the phone out of my hand. Let us know when you will be arriving, son. If your uncles want to come, and they would like to have Cabin #3, I'm sure we can make that happen. I love you, Lee."

"Love you too, mom. See you soon."

Just like that, Lee thought, *my mother told me everything I need to know.*

"Lee, how are you, son?" Thomas was emotional and Lee heard it in his voice.

"Dad, I have missed you. I do need to ask you something right away, though. And I'm almost sixteen, so I can handle the truth."

What's on your mind?"

"When I first came here with Uncle Denis and Uncle Waine, I thought it was an adventure and we were on a mission to find out where God put my mother when she died. I know she went to heaven, but we wanted to find her body. That's how I understood who we were looking for in my five-year-old mind. My uncles told me that, before we all moved to Canada, you, mom, Hope and me tried very hard to find my mother and any other living members of the 'Lee' family. As I understand it, we found no one. No 'Lee' that I might be related to. Am I all there is left of my mother's family?"

"Son, I would like us to be sitting down together when we have that discussion. Your mother's remains must be somewhere, and I believe we all need to put our heads together and retrace the steps from her death in the hospital forward. Was this the question you wanted to ask?"

"Sorry. I did get sidetracked. My question is even more personal, Dad. When I left with my uncles did you have a time in mind regarding when I would return home? I have memories of asking my uncles things like did you give me away, or did they buy me from you? That sounds totally crazy to my more mature age, but that's how confused I was as a young boy."

"Son, this is another question that is best answered when you are home with us. The short answers are that we did *not* give you away and we did *not* sell you. I think our mistake was in not discussing with you what your return plans might look like." Paradise, sitting directly in front of Thomas, was hearing the conversation in real time. "And by the way, you are *priceless,* son. No amount of money could ever 'buy' you.

"Good God, I wish that I had raised this question with you years ago. I feel so much better, and I appreciate you not laughing at this question. It seems so childish as I say it out loud today, but I was a child then and it has never left my mind."

"That's good to hear, son. And, before I continue: you might not remember this, but your mother's background makes her very protective of anyone's improper use of the word God."

"I do remember Mom yelling 'language' when anyone swore. She probably wasn't yelling other than to make sure we all heard her. I remember hearing her speak in a whisper to my uncles that she didn't condone the foul mouths they had, and that they needed to stop using this language around me. I'll get on that right away!"

"That's a good idea. On another topic, at some point you will undoubtedly ask why there have been no phone calls between us. The clinical answer is that phone calls from Cape St Mary to Honolulu are very expensive. When you left, we called all the time. I think we were overdoing it, to be honest, and not only did we run up a very expensive phone bill, but I think your uncles were made to feel that we worried they could not raise you. Paradise and I could have handled this so much better if we had taken time to prearrange our calls to prevent us leaving messages which forced your uncles to return our calls. Again, let's talk about this when you are home with us. To use your mother's vernacular, 'these items have been parked for far too long,' so how about this, Lee: you look at dates to fly home, and bring your uncles, so they will need tickets, too."

"Perfect, dad. Uncle Waine has already brought our large calendar to the table. We use it for everything important that's happening for all three of us. I love you both. Thanks for being so understanding."

"We love you, son. Hope should be home soon, so next time we speak, you can have a few minutes with your sister. She will be so happy when you come home, and I am certain she could do some homework for you regarding universities to visit."

28: Speaking in colours

During their last phone call, Ben had talked about packing everything up and coming home to the Cape. Hope had played along until he asked if she might be in Cape St Mary when he arrived home from Paris permanently.

Until that moment, the conversation had felt safe and somewhat light-hearted. At least, that's the way Hope saw it. She couldn't speak for Ben. She needed to talk with Penelope when they saw each other later that day.

"Penelope, I don't know how long I will stay in the city. Do you know what your plans are? Living here? Going back to wherever you came from? Coming home with me to the Cape? I realize your head must be spinning with all you have had to take in, but here's another thing. Ben will be moving back to the Cape, and suddenly I don't know how I feel about that. He made it clear that he is only returning because we have reconnected, and I find that frightening. Colour me confused. If you would come home with me I could use you as an excuse to not see Ben."

"Hope, my head is spinning. The only thing I know for sure is that I am not returning to Quebec. For me, that small bed-sitting room, as my landlord called the closet he rented to me, will always be associated with visits from my father, who sought me out simply to fill my head with lies about my mother. That bastard! I can truly say that I hate him, and he might be the only person I have ever truly hated."

Hope attempted to lighten the moment. "Hey, girl, tell me how you really feel!" She was relieved to hear Penelope laugh.

"Not sure how I feel having you 'use me as an excuse'. But I do have news. I have heard from Mike, and don't even ask me how on earth he tracked me down. I would like to go back to the Cape at least once to have a real 'date' with him, if you think your parents wouldn't mind me inviting myself to visit. Honest to God, Hope, I have had less than five real dates in my sad twenty-five years. Don't spread that statistic, please."

"Actually, mom gave Mike your number, after making sure that would be okay with Sydney. I suspect mom used this as a 'teach-able moment' with Sydney and she would have found a way to bring up the fact that Sydney had not allowed me to date in all the years I lived with her. I had to study 24/7 with her looking over my shoulder. It was intense. We must ensure that doesn't happen to you."

"Tell your mom it was a teachable moment of epic proportions. Early one morning, just after breakfast and out of the blue, mom shared that a young man by the name of Mike had called looking for me. She said she was surprised, maybe even shocked, that he would call the Chief Medical Examiner, which I found comical. After some discussion, mom did understand that Mike was not calling the ME for the province of Nova Scotia! God forbid. I wish you had been there, Hope. She admitted that she really assumed the call was for her and she was perhaps a bit too formal with some 'Mike' who was asking if it was possible to speak with Penelope."

"You have already accomplished more than I was able to," Hope said. "I met a couple of nice guys at university, and gave them my home number at the mansion. Somehow, Sydney intercepted those messages, and they never made it to my desk. Her driver took me to and from my classes each day. That was so my home studies could begin the moment I arrived home. And I am not kidding! To be fair, she knew nothing else."

Hope thought of all Sydney had gone through that made her the way she was "I am truly happy for Sydney, and more so for you. It must be an incredible feeling to meet your mother as you are turn-ing twenty-five years old. In retrospect I believe my packing up and leaving the mansion shocked her, but, more importantly, it softened her. I could see the softening when you did your *fainting thing* and she took control. In that moment she was acting like a mother. *Your mother.* Sydney is going to be a natural at it. I could tell as she barked instructions to the rest of us. I was incredibly proud of your mother, Penelope."

Hope could see that she made Penelope cry. She was an ugly crier, too, but Hope would keep that to herself. For now.

"One more thing, Penelope. I have had less than one date as compared to your less than five, so cry me a river!"

"I love your humour, Hope, and our long discussions. It feels like the friend I have needed during my entire life."

"Okay, this is beginning to sound like a love fest. Let's go raid the pantry for chocolate."

"One more comment, or I guess it's a question. What does "colour me confused" mean? In the short time I have known you I've heard you use many variations of the expression. Colour me happy. Colour me sad. Colour me hitched. Colour me blue—"

Hope was laughing out loud. "Okay I get it. I use *'colour me....'* way too often. I'm glad you pointed it out, though, because I haven't known you for all that long, yet you've got enough examples for me to put that expression to bed indefinitely. Just to close the conversation, 'colour me done.'"

29: Renovations

"With Lee returning home, even if it's only for a few months, I want his room to look like *his* room and not a guest room," Paradise said. She was sitting on the stoop outside, enjoying her first coffee of the day with Thomas.

"It won't be hard to do," suggested Thomas. "We can empty his room of all the 'five-year-old-kid stuff', including furniture and art-work. Painting the room a lighter colour will open it up a bit. There is space for a full-size bed and a desk befitting a university student who, we hope, will come home and use it now and then. Lee left here over a decade ago feeling very much a part of this household and we will ensure he enters that door feeling the same way."

Thomas had a few ideas, and he knew Paradise did as well. Late night discussions over the last couple of nights had been 'parked' with the promise to cement a plan on the stoop this morning.

"First things first," Paradise said, over second cups of coffee. "Pops rebuilt this house with five bedrooms in mind. Let's start there. We need our bedroom, two more for the kids, a guest room, maybe for Penelope, and an office. Did I miss anything?"

"I don't believe so, good place to begin my love. If we have a big-enough bedroom ourselves, we can incorporate an office in it. I think we should give both Lee and Hope the next two largest bed-rooms. If Hope works with us in PIU, she will need an office. Lee will need room to study and relax in his own space as well. That leaves a guest room, plus one room not yet accounted for." Thomas could see that Paradise wanted to jump in, so he was happy to sit back and enjoy his coffee.

"I agree and I disagree."

"Why am I not surprised?" Thomas knew this would be a good

discussion, perhaps even a debate.

"Just a few days ago we closed our files labelled 'bring Penelope home' and 'X', at the instruction of Sydney Scott. She wants no further activity or discussion on either file. Additionally, we have been paid in full. Agreed?"

"Agreed. However, what does this have to do with the number of bedrooms we have here at #548?"

"Stick with me. You know I sometimes like taking the long way around." Thomas could see Paradise was enjoying this, and knew where it was headed; but his partner had imagined it first, so she was in charge.

"Our last two projects were secretive to the point that, while we were working for Sydney, we weren't out in the community, therefore our names are not that familiar now. You and I will have to hustle to find work, and one of us might have to travel for work. That isn't ideal under any circumstances and more so with Lee coming home. Having said all of that, here comes my pitch." Paradise took a deep breath before she continued.

"Let's talk with Pops and see if he thinks there is one bedroom that could, more easily than the others, be extended to the outside. My thought is that, if we can grow our business, we might need an office with a door to the outside anyway, and with Hope learning the ropes by working with our local police force, there will be times when she will need to hold meetings in her office. Rather than creating offices in our bedrooms, let's see about building a PIU office that we can all use. What about inviting Pops and Eugenie to supper tonight just to have an initial discussion with them?"

"That's very in-depth thinking, my love, so let's do it. If Pops thinks a new office extension to our home will keep Hope here more often, he will build it with his bare hands!"

"I will call them. Assuming they are available and can join us, let's figure out what we will serve for supper in case we need to make a food run to the grocery store. We have lots of time." Paradise went to the kitchen, where one of their phones was located.

"I believe Hope is coming home one of these days...speaking of our grocery bills!"

Thomas wasn't sure Paradise heard him, but that was okay. When Paradise was travelling through Ontario and Quebec in pursuit of Penelope, Thomas had often spoken out loud to no one in particular.

30: Population boom

Pops was shocked. "It sounds like the population of our little Cape St Mary is increasing. Hope might be around more, and perhaps lovely Penelope as well."

They were sitting around the kitchen table at #548, at the end of a lovely meal. Eugenie, from her seat beside him, said, "I'm sure Pops would be delighted to help to make this happen."

"Paradise, this discussion takes me back to a long-ago afternoon when the sky was bluer than I had ever witnessed, and I swear the sun was bouncing along the waves in the ocean off Mavillette Beach. I saw your mother, Madeline, and my Cole walking along Cape St Mary Road straight to me, where I was sitting on the stoop, enjoying the day. I could see they were after something because they were talking 'small talk', and I had just learned what that expression meant, so I recognized it right away. Even our greetings that day were stifled. I played along."

Pops travelled back to a time before Madeline and Cole were both gone. His grandson was lost at sea, and Madeline died giving birth to Paradise.

"Back then, this house was collapsing around us, but it was my home. I bought and paid for it in cash! I had worked hard to buy this property and early on I planned to work on the house each day after fishing. A fisherman knows there is no work done after giving it your all out there on the sea.

"Anyways, I said to them, 'Now, for the love of God, why are you two fidgeting? Say what's on your mind, Cole.'"

"Finally, they unveiled their plan. It was a shocker.

"'Pops,' Cole said, 'we're getting married in the small church here in the Cape, and we would both love it if you would come with us. There is one more little thing we want to tell you. We're having a baby. Best we can figure, that will happen in about six months. Do you think we could move in with you, Pops? Then I could fish with you until the baby comes, just so we have some money in the bank by the time we become parents.'

"Finally, a few words directly from the mouth of Madeline. That girl was some shy and she spoke in such a whisper she had to repeat every word before I could figure out what she was telling me. 'Pops, I'm not much good at fixing steps, or floors or kitchen cabinet doors, but I can clean houses better than most women and I can do all the cooking and I promise to have a hot meal waiting for you and my soon-to-be husband every day that you are out at sea.'

"After a moment, I figured out what to say. 'Please hear me out and pardon me if I sound angry or emotional. I am both. Cole, all that money and time wasted going to university, and you want to fish with me? You always said you wanted to break out of the fishing jobs that consume every man in the Cape. If you start your career fishing, you will end up an old man and you will still be fishing. That is not what I want for you. It's not what you want for your family. Ask any of your relatives back on the Rock and they will confirm what I'm saying. You've completed the schooling to have a career, not a job as a fisherman, son.'

"Next, I turned on Madeline and, believe me I have kicked myself a million times since. I knew better, even back then. 'Madeline, didn't you take a fancy typing course up the line last year? Did you know you were pregnant when I gave you the money to pay for your own typewriter so you could practice your typing skills from home?'

"I saw her tears, but Cole saw them sooner and he was angry with me. 'Pops,' he said, 'you can rail on me all you want, but do *not* pick on my girlfriend. I'm stunned to hear the things coming out of your mouth'"

"I held up both hands. 'You're right, Cole. I apologize to both of you. You're a young couple, ready to take on a baby en route to taking on the world. Cole, I would love to have you as my co-captain. Madeline, I'm sure you will bring a women's touch to my home...

and, to make it official, please call it *our* home. So, when's the wedding? When are you moving in? It seems the only thing here that comes with a date is the baby.'?"

Pops turned to Paradise and said, "That's about all the 'going back in time' that I can do for now, but leave this with me. I will be back to you tomorrow or the day after that. I'm going to check down at the police station, because at least two of our local officers were instrumental in the rebuild of this place. I know we even have some floor plans somewhere. They might be hard to find, but I'll put the word out there and things will happen. Everybody seems to be kind to old Pops at this stage of my life."

Eugene saw the perfect place to speak up. "Speaking of this stage of your life, Pops, do you know what time it is? It's after one in the morning! We have no business being out this late at night."

"My darling, wife, I will take your word for it. Paradise, the meal was outstanding as usual, and the conversation seems to have gotten away from us several hours ago. I am truly sorry. I did too much thinking back to this house when I lived in it."

Hand in hand Pops and Eugenie set off to walk the short path to their home.

Paradise and Thomas decided to have a nightcap and to think about this extension to their home, with the intention to prepare a spreadsheet and figure out what things would cost so they could make a budget.

While Thomas prepared their drinks, Paradise cleared the messages on their answering machine.

There was only one long message and, as she listened to their PIU partner, Jim Taylor, a tear escaped her eye.

Thomas couldn't imagine who would have called this late, nor what had made Paradise cry.

31: What we can offer

Paradise, without saying a word, put the phone back on the wall mount in the kitchen. "I need to sit down, my love."

"What is it? Is someone sick? What is going on?" Paradise looked like she might faint right before his eyes and Thomas was more and more worried as the seconds ticked by.

"Thomas, I can hardly catch my breath. It was Jim on the phone. Jim Taylor. I saved the message so you can listen to it, but I warn you, it's very tough. In a nutshell, they were working a murder case. The victim was a young man, a boy, really. He was gay and had only recently come out to his family and close friends."

Paradise took a deep breath, stood and lifted the phone to her ear again. She engaged the message service, then handed the phone to Thomas and sat again.

He fumbled a little bit before getting the phone into position, so he missed the start of the message. But what he heard chilled him.

...Clint and I were tracking the suspect, and we followed him to an empty garage on the South side of Port Hope. Our intel assured us he was the only occupant in the building. Our intel was wrong.

There were two thugs and they opened fire the second we stepped inside. We hit both. They hit both Clint and me. They were bleeding harder and more than I was. Very little blood visible around Clint, but he was face-down and not moving.

They fled and I let them, because my total focus was on my partner. Our partner.

I turned him over. They had shot him literally between

the eyes. I have never seen anything like it.

I called an ambulance, but I knew Clint was gone.

[pause, with breathing]

We made a pact years ago that if one of us lost our life in a battle that could even remotely resemble a hate crime against gay men, the other of us would destroy all proof of our marriage. The victim's light was snuffed out by a homophobic biker who was bragging about his killing only moments after the murder. The victim's parents explained everything to us, and they were adamant that they knew who murdered their only child and they were equally adamant that he acted alone. We should have asked more questions...

Thomas hung up the phone. He said, in a shaky voice, "I'll try to listen to the rest tomorrow."

"Thomas, Jim's comment about their marriage will forever haunt me."

She drank her night-cap to the bottom of her glass, then said, "Since gay marriage is illegal there is no need for paperwork to action a divorce. Their marriage never happened. I don't know what he has to destroy."

"Pictures?" Thomas mused. "Letters...?"

"Later in the message he says he hopes to hear from us. He's not going anywhere in the next few days, but, even though the Port Hope police are keeping an eye on the office, he does not feel safe."

Thomas was on his feet. "I could fly to Toronto and then drive to Port Hope for a few days. Or do you think he would rather be alone?"

"I would prefer that we crawl into bed and at least try to sleep for a few hours. Then you should listen to the entire message in case I have forgotten something of significance. Sound good?"

Thomas agreed. "In the morning, let's take our coffee to the back stoop and think about what we can offer in terms of help for Jim.

For example, he might like to come here for a while."

"Or he might like to actually *move* here," said Paradise. "He will be expecting a call first thing in the morning, and we have lots to talk about before we call."

With a tug on Thomas's shirt, Paradise closed the loop on any further discussion as she pretended to drag him to bed. "Say goodnight, Thomas."

"Goodnight, Thomas," he said.

32: Put your business hat on

Paradise and Thomas were up before five the following morning. Needing Hope to prepare for her first case with the team, Paradise called her in Halifax just an hour later. "This better be good, mother, especially at this it's-still-very-dark-outside hour. So, who died?"

"Hope. We will call this a teachable moment. When you are working with PIU, never ever use the expression 'who died?' unless you are standing beside a body. Because someone *has* died. Should I let you get out of bed and splash cold water on your face? If Penelope is sleeping in your suite don't put me on speakerphone. Please, Hope, take thirty seconds to wake up. I need your help."

"Be back in thirty mom, don't hang up."

True to her word, Hope seemed alert and anxious when she returned in less than thirty seconds. "Talk to me, mom. I did press 'on' on my coffee pot so I will be even more alert in about two minutes. What is going on and how can I help?"

"That sounds more like you."

Paradise took a deep breath before continuing. She wished there was a way she could be delivering this terrible news in person. "Love, I have some terrible news to share. Clint and Jim were involved in a gun battle with a murder suspect they had been hunting."

"Oh my God, mother. Are they both okay?"

"Hope, *stop* interrupting me, please. We have talked about this."

"Sorry."

"Everybody got shot. Jim is wounded, and I am sorry to say that Clint has died."

The silence at the other end of the line spoke volumes.

"Clint left a message last night, and we are going to call this morning and learn more. We do know that the thugs who killed Clint had recently murdered a young man simply because he was gay." Paradise realized she had dumped a lot of information on Hope, but she would have to learn to take information like this without collapsing if she was going to work with PIU.

"Is dad standing by to make the call to Jim? I have questions but I don't want to delay it. Maybe I could be on the call too?"

"I have a few more minutes, so fire away."

"Ah, Mom, is 'fire away' any better than 'who died?' Really?"

Paradise took a second before responding. She almost had a smile on her face. "Good for you, Hope. A teachable moment came back to bite me. Now, you have one minute to ask your questions."

Hope spoke quickly. "How badly was Jim injured? Did they get the bad guys? Are we now hunting one or two murder suspects? Can I borrow one of your guns until I can afford to buy one of my own?"

"Don't get ahead of yourself. About guns: first, we practice together on the shooting range as soon as you come home. And we will go often. When your father and I think you're ready, we will give you one of our guns. Having said that, all things changed with Jim's call last night so one thing at a time. Yes, Jim was injured. But we need to talk to him to find out more." Paradise realized how unbelievably hard this would be for Hope, who was just beginning her transition to a new career.

"Mom, can I please be on the call?"

"Let me talk with your dad, and then we will let Jim make the decision."

"Thanks, mom. I totally respect that."

"If we call you, it will be within the next ten minutes and I would imagine that your dad, Jim and I will all be on the line. So, put your business hat on and use our names rather than mom and dad. You must start somewhere."

"Sure."

33: Should have done our homework

Jim Taylor answered his phone on the first ring. "Hello?"

"Hi, Jim," Thomas said. "Before we officially begin this call, are you okay if our daughter, Hope, takes part? Paradise has brought her up to date regarding your message and she very much wants to be part of this call."

"Okay."

Paradise wasn't 100% sure Jim had much interest in any part of this, but she understood why. She said, "Jim, give me one minute to add Hope."

It was less than a minute, but the silence was deafening.

"Hope d'Entremont, Private Investigator, Forensics expert...*in training.*" Hope attempted to lighten the mood by adding the '*in training.*'

Surprising both Thomas and Paradise, Jim said, "Hope d'Entremont, if you're joining PIU, you had better be adding the 'Unstructured' part of our name to your salutation. It's Private Investigators *Unstructured,* young lady. Got that?" Paradise was sure she heard a smile...a silent smile.

"Point taken. PIU it is." Hope was being all official. Paradise could imagine her saluting.

Thomas said, "Jim, let me say, on behalf of Hope, Paradise and me, while we are grieving our own loss of Clint, we acknowledge that he was much more than a fellow PI to you. We are so very sorry for your loss. Do you want to begin with a recap of the message you left us last night? It might be a good place to begin for everyone. And, for reference as we move forward with this murder case/hate crime, I will now hit the 'record' button."

"Sounds okay, and I'll do the best I can on virtually no sleep during the last 24 hours. Clint and I received a call from a Mr. Doyle Alexander, the father of a deceased man we had read about in our local paper. Newsworthy because this twenty-five-year-old man, David Alexander, was gay. Even our local paper spoke unkindly of this man simply because of his life choices. They used a nasty slur during the article. The paper decreased the font size of the slur, possibly thinking many would not read it. Clint and I saw it as bold highlighting of the author's words. Young David had just recently shared his lifestyle with his parents. They were supportive, as I think he knew they would be. His father, Doyle, told Clint and me that he cried listening to his son share how he had been bullied in school, and now at work. David worked in finance and three of his co-workers had followed him into a gay bar and taunted him in front of everyone. Only a couple of his friends stood by him. The others didn't want to be part of 'it', as they called the bullying, so they kept their mouths shut.

"I need to say that Mr. Alexander hired us only four days ago. He was so certain that he knew precisely who had murdered his son. He gave us his name the first time we spoke, and he was convinced the man had acted alone.

"Mr. Alexander called us numerous times per day, asking for a 'status report.' Looking back, Clint and I did not do sufficient research. We listened to Mr. Alexander too often and for too long each time he called. He even invited us over 'for a drink or two.' We declined. The man had just lost his only child, and we were prepared to make a few concessions because we felt deeply for him and more so for his murdered son. However, we agreed that having a drink in his home at this time might be too much. Professionalism first. Always first."

"Speaking of drink," Hope said in a whisper, "I'm parched just listening to your story, Jim, so you must need a drink of something."

"Thanks, I did forget to hit the 'on' button of my coffee pot, but I can almost stretch and hit it if you would just give me a second. Clint always made the coffee."

Jim's voice broke for a second, but he recovered and continued.

"Hope, I didn't realize how dry my mouth has become until you suggested I might be parched. I would like to continue but I don't want to do all the talking. I'll be as brief as I can."

"No need to be brief," Hope said. "We want to hear everything you have the energy to share."

"The night of the stakeout we approached the abandoned gas station. We entered by the only door available to us and that might have been the ambush. Every gas station has more than one door, for Christ's sake, and we should have known that. We did not complete our homework before heading out. Mr. Alexander was so positive this thug acted alone.

There were two men, high atop the hoist used to jack cars up so mechanics can work on the underbelly of a car. They waited until we were fully inside the building, guns drawn, and probably looking like idiots to them. In an instant, both Clint and I were shot. I still didn't realize there were two shooters. I think Clint was dead before he hit the floor.

"I managed to shoot both but, as they fell silent, I was more worried about Clint than I was in making sure they were dead. I still don't know which one escaped. At least I got one of them. Initially it looked like there was blood from both shooters but there is no record of anybody going to emergency with gunshot wounds.

"The local police called me during the night to advise they found one body near the back of the gas station. They know I'm alone in our building, and I shared with our local police chief that I am not sure I can stay here. Can I turn this over to you three now, please? My tank is empty."

Thomas spoke. "Jim, would you like me to come and spend some time with you? We could review the outstanding files you have to see if anything stands out that might be related to this case; we *will* find Clint's murderer, and we will do that together, I promise you. Paradise, I'm not sure if you or Hope need to come immediately."

"It's my turn, Jim," said Paradise. "Not today but down the road, you might want to sell the building. We would all be in on that transaction of course but I think we would be prepared to take direction from you. Please consider coming here for a while, just to remove yourself from that scene. Or move here permanently. Honestly, Jim, this is an incredible place to live. You can stay with us for however long you like, and if you want to, we will take you house hunting."

"My turn," said Hope. "Jim, don't do anything as drastic as moving right away. I'm sure you and Clint have made wonderful memories in that building so make sure you have taken the time to pack those memories up before you leave."

"Jim," Thomas said, "I'm not sure how our daughter got so smart, but she makes an excellent point. Can I wrap this up for now? You know you can call us any time, day or night. I'm going to see how soon I can get to Toronto, and I will rent a car there and come straight to you."

Jim seemed tearful as he spoke. "I would much rather pick you up at the airport, Thomas. In fact, I have two cars sitting here, and you can help me get rid of one. Additionally, on our drive back I can bring you up to date on pretty much everything."

"It's a date. I will give you my arrival time later this evening. Fair warning: if I can get a seat on the red-eye tonight, I will be with you before you know it. Take it easy for a day or two, Jim, but keep in touch with Mr. Alexander. He might have some information on where the second shooter might be hiding out. Call him, though… don't go to his home. Stay inside if you can."

~

The phone rang almost as soon as Paradise hung it up, with Hope on the line.

"Hi, Hope. Dad and I are very happy with your contribution to our conversation. You will bring the human touch to PIU. Especially right now when the human touch is somewhat fractured for Jim."

"Thanks, Mom. This won't take long. Why don't you drive to the airport with dad, and I will pick you up and bring you back here for the night. I thought we could spend a few hours tomorrow with

Sydney and Penelope and then drive home together. Would you mind?"

"I would not mind at all, and I love the idea. During our windshield time en route back to the Cape I can bring you up to date on the construction underway to enlarge our home to create an official office. Oh, and one more thing. Your brother is coming home for a couple months!"

"Lee is coming home? Oh my God, mother, that is incredible news. He's coming home at exactly the right time to bring a smile to our faces. Let's celebrate the decade of birthdays we have missed. More than a decade, I suspect."

"I have to go and pack a few things and break the news to you father that he is not driving to the airport solo."

Thomas chimed in. "Hope, don't pick your mother up because we don't want to leave my car at the airport. I might be longer than planned. Mom can drive to the mansion. Ask Sydney if she has an extra parking spot where we could leave a car, doesn't matter which one."

"Good thinking, dad. Mom can park where I usually park, so not a problem. I will mention it to Sydney, though. I love you both."

34: As long as it takes

"Sweetheart," Thomas said over the phone, "normally I would ask if you would *like* to fly to Toronto, but I don't have that luxury. You have knowledge about the world of forensics that your mother and I have not delved into. So, like it or not, I *need* you to fly to Toronto."

"Dad, I will take my first step in my PI journey with this case, and you can give me anything to do, no matter how small, and you can give me a gun—"

"Capital 'N' Capital 'O.' NO. End of that discussion. If we have time away from the case, I will take you to a shooting range. Possibly Jim could take you as well. But understand that you will not have a gun in your hand unless you are with one of us. Understood?" Thomas hoped the discussion wouldn't come up every time he, Paradise, or Jim had to be armed.

"Oh. My. God. Dad, it was only a joke."

"Sure."

"Okay, Dad, you never offer one-word answers so now I know you are really upset with me. I give you my word. I won't bring it up again. Promise."

"Thank you, Hope."

"Sure."

Hope continued packing and getting herself ready for a midnight flight to Toronto with her dad. She couldn't remember if they had ever gone on such an important trip. Certainly, she had not. He had suggested she inform Sydney about their plans. Penelope would want to know what had happened, where she was going and when she would be back.

~

Thomas kept his attention on driving…it was very dark along some of the country roads. They had travelled this route numerous times when they were both working for Sydney. That seemed like a hundred years ago.

Paradise focused on lists for each of the three of them. Some of Hope's things that were in Halifax. She had wanted to take them home to the Cape, and Paradise could do that for her.

For herself, Paradise's list contained talking with Pops about the office addition to their home; calling Lee to let him know that his dad and Hope might be away for a couple of weeks; sitting down with Eugenie and Pops and perhaps Wilmot and Marie at the same time…in fact, she would call them from Halifax and invite them to dinner as soon as she had a better idea of when that could be.

Her second list was for Hope, and it was more of a checklist for reviewing what Hope had packed for the trip, just in case she might have forgotten something she would 'really, really' wish she had taken. That often happened to Hope as she went back and forth between the Cape and the city.

"Thomas, when you're ready let's talk about your list to be completed while you are in Port Hope with Jim. I'll greenlight and you can jump in at any time. I will leave it to you and Jim to prioritize each item once you are settled and you feel Jim is ready for the conversation."

Thomas seemed upset. "First and before any damn list, Jim and I will hunt down and capture the thug who murdered our partner. We owe it to Clint to make this our top priority every day and as long as it takes."

"Of course, my love. This list is for *after* you have taken care of business…finding Clint's killer. God, I cannot imagine how Jim must be feeling right now. He seemed totally lost when we talked, didn't you think?"

"Yes. That's a good word for it. Jim is lost in a world where such hate towards a young gay man ends in murder. Let's work with your list for a bit of time. I can't be crying while driving and you're worse, so don't be offering to switch places."

"Understood. Here we go:

1. Talk with Jim about his mental health.
2. Compile and review all files in the office, both closed and active.
3. Prioritize files and ensure those files at the top of the pile are acted on. Some of these will be projects Hope can work on for you.
4. Ask Jim if he would consider packing up everything and moving to the Cape. Initially he should live with us. Might be a bit crowded, but we will do it in memory of Clint. We can find Jim a nice little home. A yearly lease on one of the beautiful cottages right on the Cape, for example.
5. You and Jim should have a long talk, with Hope listening in and bringing that extra voice to the discussion, about selling our building in Port Hope. I know we should wait a year, but once we load up all the files, if that is what happens, is it safe to leave our building vacant, given what has happened?

"Paradise, when we make lists, we don't try to solve every issue before moving on to the next. We greenlight, remember? This list we have started is perfect but let's keep it simple. If I use the last item, you spoke about, as an example, number 5 could say, 'Discuss the future of our Port Hope real estate.' But, for now it's all about Jim. No one else."

"Right you are. I need a break anyway."

Paradise reached over to rub Thomas's shoulder. She was frightened for him, and for Hope too, flying to Toronto and not really understanding what had happened and where to go from here.

She knew her husband would protect their daughter. But what would they face?

35: A note on the desk

It didn't take long before the 'Cape reno team' was revitalized and raring to go. Most of the boys who had rebuilt Pops' old home, of which only the façade could be salvaged, were once again by his side.

When the time was right, Pops had, lovingly, passed the house on to Thomas, Paradise, Lee and Hope. The renovation would be in good hands with Pops as project manager, contract manager, and general manager all rolled into one. He loved his phony titles, and his 'team' loved using all his titles when addressing him.

Holding Eugenie's hand, Pops reached out to knock at "the kids'" back door. Excitement was brewing and he couldn't wait. He had his opening speech ready and was relatively certain the kids would approve. And if they didn't, Pops and his men would make some changes, and try for approval again.

"I'm telling you Pops, there is no one home," Eugenie said. "Their car left, I think it was yesterday, with both Thomas and Paradise inside, and no one has come back since. Something is going on with those two. You know they never leave the Cape without touching base to let us know when they will be back. I watched from the kitchen window because I just happened to be sitting at the kitchen table. They didn't take much luggage, but it was more than that. They weren't looking at each other and I don't think they were doing much talking, either. Something is wrong, Pops. I feel it."

"I know you said that, sweetheart, but it's not like them to leave in a rush without letting us know what's going on. And if they are away, they would have left a note on the kitchen table for us."

Figuring he had knocked enough, Pops opened the door and

they stepped cautiously in.

Eugenie saw it first. "Pops there is a note on the desk. I bet it's for us."

"It better be, because I have a date today with my reno team and we need a few guidelines before we begin. Everyone on the team has ideas to share with Thomas and me. We really want to get started, preferably while they're away, as they seem to be now, but do we take that chance knowing we don't have a sign-off from them?" Suddenly Pops wasn't as sure of himself as he normally was.

Both stood looking at the note and, knowing Pops was a bit of a slow reader, Eugenie spoke up. "It's longer than their usual notes. Pops, why don't you check around, including upstairs, while I see what this note is about." Eugenie had a good idea, but wasn't ready to discuss it with Pops.

"I'm not looking for anyone who might be injured or dead am I?" Pops had lost his confidence. Eugenie was noticing this more and more often.

Pops was upstairs and back down before Eugenie had fully digested the note. She had read enough to know something was terribly wrong. She stopped reading at that point and waited for Pops to sit down beside her.

"Everything upstairs looks normal to me. Hope's room is a mess, but when isn't it a mess?" Pops smiled as he looked at his wife. His smile quickly left his face. "God, what is it? I knew something was wrong. I've had this feeling since last night when there were no lights on here. Not a one."

"Sit with me," said Eugenie as she patted the seat beside her. "Our little family is just fine, Pops, but there has been an incident involving their PI partners in Ontario."

"Read it to me. Every word." Pops had gone white as a sheet and Eugenie worried for him. His health had been declining over the last couple of years.

Eugenie took Pops' hand as she began.

Dear Pops and Eugenie,
We are off to Halifax in a rush to hopefully get Thomas on

the midnight flight to Toronto. There has been a horrific crime in Port Hope, Ontario. There is no easy way to share this. Our partners, Clint and Jim, were hired to hunt a murderer. Clint was shot and later died. Jim was wounded.

Jim is not doing well, so Thomas and Hope are going to stay with him for a while.

I will be back here tomorrow unless I end up going with them. If I don't return tomorrow, I will call to let you know where we all are and what's going on.

Pops, Thomas has asked me to remind you that you're in charge of the reno. Perhaps for now, you could mark the recommended changes on the ground outside of our home so we can see where we will be adding space.

Pops and Eugenie, we love you both...so much.

Looking directly at Pops, Eugenie was even more worried about him. Perhaps the 'bad feeling' she had was related to her husband, not Paradise and Thomas.

"Pops, please *do not* give me a hard time about this...come with me. I want you to lie down for a minute before we walk home. There is something going on in that body of yours. How are you feeling?"

"Not good," came the reply.

After she got Pops as comfortable as she could make him on the couch, Eugenie ran for help...muttering the Stations of the Cross. Her rosary was always around her neck.

36: Wherever you are

With Hope and Thomas in the air, flying to Toronto, Paradise had just said goodnight to Sydney and Penelope. As she entered the Halifax apartment that she and Hope had shared for so many years, she heard the phone ring.

"Hello?"

"Hello? Hello? Hello? Is that you, Hope?"

"I'm sorry, I can't hear you. Can you speak slower and louder, if you can? How can I help you?"

"Hope?"

"Hope is not here right now. I'm her mother, Paradise. Can I take a message?"

"Oh, thank the Lord. Paradise, this is Eugenie. Pops is in an ambulance for Halifax and I'm so scared. I'm such a mess."

Paradise sat down. "Eugenie, what happened? Please continue to speak slowly. You're doing great. I know you're frightened. I'm frightened, too. Can you tell me exactly when this happened?"

Clarity had returned to Eugenie, and she was much easier to follow. "Paradise, I just know my husband is dead." Paradise thought Eugenie might be in shock. Maybe she could get some answers if she asked one thing at a time. "Eugenie, did Pops fall?"

"No."

"I'm in Halifax. If an ambulance is bringing Pops to one of the hospitals here, I can find him. I will call you as soon as I find him. How does that sound?"

"That would be wonderful. I would appreciate it so much, and I feel better just knowing he will be with you. Do I have time to tell you what happened, or do you have to leave to be meet him?"

"Give me the highlights of what happened and as soon as I see

Pops, or as soon as I find out what is going on, I'll come to bring you into the city so you can be with him. Eugenie, are you sure the paramedics told you they were taking Pops to Halifax? They might take him to Kentville."

"I'm so sorry, Paradise. Yes, I believe they did say Kentville, but they said they would let me know for sure what hospital my Pops would be in. I don't think they asked for my phone number, though, so how will they let me know? What a mess. Do you think he's dead, Paradise? I haven't seen too many dead people, but Pops sure looked like he was dead. How will we find out where he is? If he's dead, I don't want him to be alone."

As soon as they hung up, Paradise called her brother and his wife, Wilmot and Marie, and asked them to go and sit with Eugenie until Paradise could get home to her. All Cape residents live 'next-door' to each other and she knew her brother would be at Pops and Eugenie's door in just a few minutes.

Paradise immediately called the Kentville hospital, identified herself and asked if Pops d'Entremont (she realized she didn't know his first name!) had been admitted. She explained that he might have passed away so the morgue would be a second place to look for Pops.

The clerk, Lorraine, agreed to call Paradise back as soon as possible.

If Pops was alive, and if the plan had always been to bring him to Halifax, he wouldn't arrive for a couple of hours. Paradise didn't have any contacts in the Halifax hospitals, so if he wasn't in Kentville she would go to the nearest emergency department to see if she could get some answers. She prayed that Lorraine would call back soon.

"Pops, I hope you can hear me, wherever you are. I'm nervous and I'm anxious, so here I am needing to talk with you...as always. You were my confidant and friend when I first moved to Cape St Mary in search of my mother and father. Your heart was breaking and so was mine the day you had to tell me that both my parents were deceased. You were so kind and gentle as you delivered the sad news. I could hardly believe my mother died giving birth to me.

That still haunts me, but I'm forever grateful that you told me. If you are with the Lord now, you will also be with your beloved grandson, Cole d'Entremont.

"Pops, the day we sat on your boat, and you let your mind wander back to the day you were out fishing with Cole, and he fell overboard and was lost at sea, I was in awe of your strength, both physical and mental. Sharing such intimate detail is never easy. You cried as much telling me the story about the death of 'your Cole' as I suspect you cried the day he fell overboard, leaving you to get yourself back to the dock and your life back to the future… whatever that future would look like for you and for everyone who knew Cole."

Paradise wondered if she would be at ease speaking with Pops like this if she learned that he really had passed away. And how would she tell Eugenie?

37: Don't worry about us

Eugenie, a former nun, turned to the Lord in her time of pain. Her beloved Pops was likely dead on the sofa even before the paramedics arrived.

She wondered why they didn't leave with their flashing lights on and siren blaring, but she learned that, because Pops was gone, there was no reason to use the lights. That awful thought had not crossed Eugenie's mind as she asked the paramedics to be careful with her husband.

The paramedics called Kentville to identify they were delivering a body to the morgue to be transported to Halifax. They gave details from the card they found in Pops' wallet and asked that someone call Eugenie d'Entremont, wife of the deceased, as soon as possible. The policy called for news relating to the death of a loved one to be given in person, but the paramedic admitted that they had gotten 'very lost' trying to find the Cape, and then Cape St Mary Road and the right house, and that was during the day, so nighttime would be so much worse.

They also shared that the widow said that she had been a nun prior to marrying Pops, so she would be speaking a lot with her Lord. As she put it, "Don't you boys be after worrying about me. I've got the Lord right here with me and his will is as it must be. I can accept that. I would ask that I hear from someone quickly, please. I'll be 'some anxious', as my Pops would put it."

~

Paradise answered the phone while it was still ringing. She hoped it would be the Kentville hospital with news. With good news, she hoped.

"Hello?"

"Paradise, it's Wilmot. Marie and I are here with Eugenie, and she is doing just fine. Have you heard from anyone?"

"No, I have not and to be honest I was hoping this call was from the Kentville hospital with news. I asked them specifically to—"

"Sister, dear, I am sorry for interrupting you."

"You never call me sister, or, at least, not since we were pre-teens. What are you not telling me?"

"I need you to just let me talk, Paradise. Please don't interrupt until I finish, okay?"

Paradise could only nod, hoping her brother would realize that she had done so rather than saying, 'Okay.'

"Eugenie has asked that I give you this news. She is sitting directly in front of me, and we both know that if I screw up, she will correct me, right, Eugenie?"

There was a rattling sound as the phone changed hands, and then Paradise heard Eugenie.

"My good lord, the two of you are making me crazy bantering back and forth. Paradise, there is no easy way to say this so I will just say it. Pops is dead. He has left this earth and I'm sure he is already with his God. As you know, Pops might have had a God somewhat different from mine! And that's okay...I'm smiling a bit, Paradise, and thank you so much for calling your brother and Marie. They ran over so fast they hadn't figured out what to say when I opened the door. They both looked like they were seeing a ghost, so perhaps it was Pops. What do you think?"

"Eugenie, I think you are remarkable. Putting us in our place, using silly phrases here and there while I know your heart is breaking. I asked the Kentville hospital to call me so I could be the one to share this devastating news with you."

"Paradise, I am not remarkable. My heart is not breaking. This news is not devastating. I have loved two men...the Lord and my Pops. When I left the convent and came home to the Cape, I certainly was not looking for a man. Pops was a gift from the Lord. How selfless was that? As husband and wife, Pops and I had a wonderful life. I think the price I will pay for having such a great love is that I will therefore suffer a great loss. However, as you know, Pops was very elderly. He had a hard time just getting out of bed each morning. We didn't speak of death, because he would have no part in such a discussion other than to remind me how much younger I am, which should mean he would die first. This is all stuff we can talk about when you come home."

"I'll be home by the time you wake up tomorrow morning," said Paradise.

"Oh, no, you absolutely will not. I won't hear of it. Wilmot and Marie and, yes, little Rescuee, are all going to spend the night here with me. They are insisting and so I have admitted that it would be nice to not wake up to an empty house in the morning."

"Tell my brother you don't feel like making a big breakfast in the morning and they need to take you out. I'm serious, Eugenie."

"You leave the morning to us. Oh, a favour, Paradise, and I'm hoping you will understand: we left your place in a bit of a mess, but I don't think I can go back there right away. Pops insisted he had to go over and measure some part of the house that he wanted to take to the next 'Re548' meeting for your renovations. He was checking out some rooms upstairs and when he came back down-stairs, I made him lie down on your sofa. I truly feel that's where and when he died."

Paradise heard some quiet chatter, and then Wilmot had the phone again.

"Paradise, when Marie and I leave Eugenie sometime tomorrow morning she wants to be alone for twenty-four hours. Specifically, she does not want you rushing back here tomorrow. She knows you had plans to check in with Doctor Scott and Penelope. And, of course, with Thomas and Hope. She did give us permission to walk with her if we see her at Mavillette Beach. We know what time they normally walk, so we will be ready to go, and so will Rescuee. Please don't worry about any of us here in the Cape. We will all be together, if that's what it takes to have a proper send-off for Pops. In fact, that's exactly what Marie and I will plan. We will run it all past Eugenie, so don't you worry about anything. Got that, sister?"

"Thank you, Wilmot, and please thank Marie for me. I will see you both soon...but not tomorrow."

38: She amazes me all the time

Jim had picked Thomas and Hope up at the Toronto International airport. Not much talking during the drive to the office.

"I hope you both had a nice sleep while I chauffeured you to our humble offices here in Port Hope," he said. "So much for bringing you up to date concerning our murder case here in this quiet little town."

As the three got out of the car, Jim added, "While you were in the air, I received a call from Paradise. It was a casual conversation with her saying all the right things about my future with PIU. She was incredibly kind, and I was touched. Hope, that's quite the mom you've got there."

"She amazes me all the time," Hope said through a yawn.

Jim turned to Thomas. "She called a second time and said she needed you to call her as soon as possible. She asked me to wait until we were all safely back at my place and *then* give you the message to call home. In that second call, Paradise did not sound like the same lady who had called previously. During the second call she seemed to be talking much slower. If she needs you to fly back right away, I will understand. I might follow you in the not-too-distant future. I don't know whether I'm coming or going, to be truthful, but the fog has left my brain for now.

To Hope, he said, "Let's get you settled upstairs. We can give your dad a bit of privacy."

To Thomas, Clint added, "Use this office, Thomas, and yell if you need anything from us while you're on the phone."

Hope was a million miles away with her own thoughts, being somewhat stunned by a day of travel. "Sorry, Jim. I zoned out for a second but I'm with you now." Jim took the steps *three at a time* and therefore Hope had to do the same. Under her breath she muttered, 'Please, God, don't tell me this pain searing up the back of my leg means I have pulled a ligament or something just to keep up with Jim."

"Kid, you're muttering and you're limping. Are you okay?"

"Never better. Can I have the apartment with the better view?"

Downstairs, Thomas had familiarized himself with the main floor including the small apartment. He wasn't sure it was to be his apartment, so he unpacked just enough to mark his territory. Next, he sat down to call Paradise. It was unlike her to call him unless it was an emergency and since he and Hope had just flown here because there was already an emergency, Thomas had no idea what was up as he placed his call home.

39: Oh, the stories!

Thomas knew Paradise had a knack of picking up the receiver at the exact time it started to ring. Smiling, he thought of the many times, sitting beside Paradise at home, when he watched her answer the phone before it had made a sound.

"Hello, Thomas. Is this you?"

"I'm here, my love, I'm here. Are you okay?"

"I'm fine. I didn't mean to frighten you with my message. Did you and Hope have a good flight, and did you get any sleep at all?"

"Not on the flight, but we did sleep all the way to Port Hope, giving Jim something to hold over us since he was hoping to discuss Clint's murder. On the plane to Toronto we were both wide awake, so Hope asked if I could teach her 'some PI stuff', as she put it. We did that for the whole trip. Our daughter's brain is like a sponge, Paradise. I began to quiz her around the time we were told to prepare for landing, and she answered every question 100% correct. She wasn't hesitant at all. I used actual case files belonging to PIU as there was no one sitting anywhere near us on the plane. I knew we had total confidentiality. If anything, Hope is far too anxious to learn to properly shoot a gun and have one of her own. I might have thrown you under the bus on that one, because I told her that topic is between Hope and you."

Thomas paused to take a drink of water, thinking Paradise might jump into the discussion. She didn't, which told him she had something serious on her mind.

"Paradise, Jim thought that when you called the second time it seemed somewhat urgent that he give me your message."

"I hate to tell you this over the phone. Pops has died. Massive heart attack, the doctor said. Thank God Eugenie was with him at the time. The doctor told Eugenie that Pops didn't suffer for one second. Wilmot and Marie are spending the night with her, so she won't be alone. She told me just a bit ago she plans to make a 'nice big breakfast' for Wilmot and Marie, as much as I know they would rather just go home and have their normal breakfast, which I believe is toast with peanut butter."

"Sweetheart, this is such terrible timing. I'm sorry I am not there with you. I think you should invite Eugenie to move into our house for a few days, or longer if that's what she needs. What do you think?"

Reeling from the news, Thomas knew this would be a difficult death for Paradise to cope with. Pops had been everything to Paradise and he understood why. Pops was the one who explained to Paradise that her mother, Madeline, had died giving birth to her. And the note...there was always talk about the blood-stained note that said everything, in only four words: 'her name is Paradise.' Pops had kept that note, although he wasn't sure why. The day he actually met Paradise; he realized he had kept the note for her.

"Thomas, as much as that would be the best way, I thought I would offer to bunk in with her for a few days. We can grieve together and laugh together, too. Can you imagine all the brilliant stories involving Pops that we need to capture? *Oh, the stories!* So many things to consider. I'm already making notes in a journal. I picked one of my new journals because there are a million lists I want to make. That's what Eugenie and I will work on."

Her voice sounded lighter.

"I wonder if Pops and Eugenie discussed their funerals," Thomas said. "I'm confident Eugenie wants a proper Catholic funeral consisting of 'only the basics' for the funeral mass, but does she know what Pops' wishes were?"

"Would you mind if we pick this up tomorrow or the next day? I am deep in grief myself, and while I thought that talking about making lists would be helpful, I think I should park all the work we will need to manage until I have cried my eyes out. Not literally, of course, but I am a bit depressed tonight and exhausted, too. Can you tell?"

"I can tell, my love. When will you return to our home? You don't have any business with Doctor Scott at the moment, correct? Did you consider driving home last night or maybe you realized you would need a good night's sleep so you can drive home in the morning. If so, that's a great idea. You sleep well and we can talk tomorrow at any time."

Thomas heard the disconnect at the other end. Knowing Paradise often ended calls this way, he didn't take it personally. He laughed at himself, realizing he had been with his wife for so long, he knew how she answered a call and how she ended it.

40: Modified master map

Lee, Uncle Denis and Uncle Waine were off to the mainland. Next stop, Toronto. The next 'next stop' would be Halifax. Finally, the last stop would be Cape St Mary in Nova Scotia, Canada! No airport in the Cape but it was a lovely drive to and from the city.

Lee had no memory of that drive, but his uncles sure did. They were anxious to pick up the rental and surprise everyone in the Cape. That's all they talked about after they had reviewed the itinerary over breakfast just before they left for the Honolulu airport.

Lee marvelled at the way they would present every trip over their first meal of the day. Details, including their actual tickets, all laid out. He knew how proud his uncles were to plan all 'family trips', as they called their outings, and to present the news to Lee only when they had taken care of everything.

Denis had called Russ at the Cape View Motel and Cottages and secured Cabin #3 for as long as they wanted it. Russ was generous with Lee's uncles once again. No money would exchange hands. They would work for their keep, so to speak.

Russ trusted Waine and Denis with his entire business. "For you and your brother, rates for cabin #3 are fixed to the same as last time, even though that was a decade ago as noted beside your names in the ledger. That also means we three are at least ten years older. Not sure how much longer I will keep the place. Staff is hard to find and working the front desk and cleaning all the rooms and having them ready when our next guests arrive is just too much for me since I lost my wife to cancer, and that's all I'll say about Carole. Pitch in when you can. No clock. No one watching over your shoulders. We will be honoured to have you stay with us again. It will be good for everyone to have you back. Your bill is forever paid in full."

The uncles kept it to themselves that Russ had also mentioned he could be talked into selling the large two-bedroom cottage closest to Cape St Mary Road, as well as the much smaller 'A' frame cottage. Denis and Waine made sure Russ understood they would like to see both cabins upon their arrival.

Lee wanted to surprise his parents and his sister, hoping they would all be home when he arrived. He realized he was taking a chance, thinking they might all be home, but his heart was set on just walking in, all these years later.

Because they had no idea when they would arrive Lee decided he would call Pops and let him know they were on their way home. He would bunk in with his uncles for the first night just to be sure Pops had had enough time to 'round 'em up,' as Pops would say, once they were on the ground in the Cape.

Safely on the ground in Toronto, the trio was just in time to board their connector flight to Halifax. There, they faced a bit of a mix-up at the car rental place and so, for the same amount of money, they were driving what Waine called 'a boat.'

"Do not insult our ride, Waine," Denis said. "This, I will have you know, is the current year's Jeep Wrangler. We will ride in style. Not only do these windows come off, but these doors come totally off, too. Pray for warm and sunny weather, boys."

At the last minute, the boys decided to rent a hotel room close to the airport and spend the rest of the day and night stretched out and studying their map of Nova Scotia. Lee oversaw the mapping out their trip to the Cape, and the second they were all comfortable in their overpriced hotel room he brought out the map.

"Gentlemen, may I have your attention please. *This* is our master map." Lee was greatly exaggerating the work he had taken in the development of this 'modified master map', as he called it.

"I will ask each of you to study your copy of this map and come to me with any questions you might have. Denis when we leave here in the morning, I propose that I be your guide from our hotel to cabin #3. I will be the keeper of our map." Lee was almost laughing out loud as he concluded his presentation.

Waine was quick to speak up. "Lee, or perhaps I should call you Sir Lee, I wholeheartedly support your proposal to guide my brother through the province. That also means you will need to ride shotgun. I am happy to lounge in the back seat, snacks by my side, soda can in my hand and feet up if I need a nap."

With a cheeky grin Lee accepted the shotgun position.

"Is it okay if I call Pops while we're relaxing just to let him know we will be home, likely, at some point tomorrow? I really want to surprise my family, and Pops is the one to help me pull it off."

Waine was proud to answer that question. "Of course it's okay, Lee. You know you never have to ask if you can call your family."

Lee checked his little black book, in which, under 'P', he had written 'Pops' all those years ago when he was five and going on an adventure with his uncles. Then, their goal had been to find his mother...his birth mother.

41: Who is the tallest?

Lee made the call and the answer was quick.

"Hello?"

Lee hadn't really prepared for this call. "Too late now," he mumbled to himself. He wondered if it was possible that no one would remember him.

"Hi, Pops. That didn't sound like you. I've heard you answer your phone many times and you never answer with just one word. Everything okay in your part of the world? Is Eugenie okay?" Lee paused to take a sip of his pop.

'This is not Pops. It's Wilmot. Who is this?"

"Wilmot as in Paradise's sister?"

"Yes, Paradise is my sister, and I will ask again…who is this?"

"Sorry, I hardly remember you. It's Lee, I've been in Honolulu, Hawaii for at least a decade. I think I was four or five when we left. Is Pops there and may I speak with him, please? I know he will remember me."

Lee heard muffled sounds followed by a female voice. It was clear, for whatever reason, he didn't seem to be able to speak with Pops.

"Lee, is it really you, dear?"

Lee was getting frustrated speaking with everyone except the man he was so eager to speak with. He didn't reply to her question…whoever she was.

"For the love of God, may I please speak with Pops? My uncles and I will arrive home late tomorrow afternoon and I really want this to be a surprise for mom and dad as well my sister. I can't wait to see Hope."

"Lee, it's Wilmot again. I am so sorry to have to give you such sad news, especially over the phone."

"Oh no." Lee ran over to the couch. "Wilmot, don't worry about me. I am sitting between my uncles, and they are going to listen to your sad news with me. Please just spit it out."

"Lee, Pops is dead. He had a massive heart attack and died instantly. Eugenie was with him. If you will let me, I can help you surprise your parents. Your mother will be happy to see you. If you're arriving tomorrow, your mother might be the only one home, but we can talk about that when you arrive."

"I will go to #3 with my uncles and call you from there. We will be home tomorrow, guaranteed. I don't feel like talking any more right now. Is that alright?"

"Lee, don't hang up just yet. Eugenie is right here. She is asking to talk to you. Can you stay on the line for a few more minutes?"

"Wilmot, it's Denis, Uncle Denis to the young man sitting right beside me. You are on speaker phone. I would love to speak with Eugenie."

"Denis, Eugenie here, it is so nice to hear your voice, and I am so happy to hear you are coming home. In many ways your timing is perfect. We are going to need reasons to smile over the next few days and weeks. We haven't even thought about when our funeral for Pops will be. This has all just happened. You three get a good night's sleep and call us when you arrive in #3, as you call it. Lee I am so sorry we must dump this terrible news on you at a time in your life when you are so happy to be coming back to the Cape. We won't mention your arrival to anyone. We will pick up some groceries for you tomorrow, so you don't run the risk of being seen before we get you home. Wilmot will help you surprise Paradise. Give me a second to grab a Kleenex. I'll be right back."

Lee and his uncles sat silently.

Eugenie was able to regain her composure quickly. "Lee, sweetheart, I am so happy you are coming home. Pops will be looking down on you and he will be so grateful that you arrived home at such a critical time in the lives of our family. We love you sweetheart and guess what? We love your uncles, too. Now, go to bed… that's an order."

Lee leaned into the phone and said, "Eugenie, thank you for being you. I can't wait to see you. You might not recognize me. I am not as big as my uncles in terms of weight, but guess who is the tallest of our trio. That would be me!"

42: What have I missed?

Hope hit the ground running after a ten-hour sleep. She could hear her dad and Jim talking downstairs.

She listened to make sure they were talking PIU and not personal stuff. It all seemed personal with Jim having lost his partner. Murdered, no less. Hope realized she was super emotional and so sad.

She splashed cold water on her face again before facing her dad and Jim. Wanting to, one day, be treated as an equal partner with PIU, she silently told herself to 'suck it up.'

"Good morning, guys. What have I missed?"

Thomas spoke up. "Hope, we are having a very general discussion about the state of PIU here in our Canadian offices."

"Really, Dad? One of our own has been murdered and you were talking 'state of the office'? I don't believe you. I really want to be a part of this team, starting today. I realize I have to learn the ropes, be a bit of a go-fer at times, and I know I won't be riding shotgun in solving Clint's murder, but please let me be part of all discussions that go on in this office. Dad, you don't have to filter anything, I promise."

"Duly noted, but allow me this *teaching moment*, as your mother calls what I am about to say." Thomas spoke to her not as a dad, but as a colleague. "There will be cases that you will not be working on. Full stop. Jim and I won't necessarily be working on the same cases either. We will learn as we go, we won't intentionally keep you in the dark, Hope, and we are always open to your input."

Thomas turned to their partner. "Jim, the floor belongs to you."

"Hope, I'm thrilled you are joining PIU. I remember my first day here. Clint interviewed me and later that same day he hired me. It's important to me that we include Clint in our discussions. I'm not bringing a Ouija board to work, but I think you both need to hear this. It won't make me cry (much) when a discussion brings on a 'Clint story.' It will help all of us heal. I will admit that in this moment, the second I wake up, my mind goes directly to Clint's murder and murderer, and I would like us to focus on that today. Everything else in this office can wait. Homicide with the local police is expecting us to meet with them down at the station as soon as we are ready. We've already lost one day. Hope, right or wrong I could not let Clint lie on that cold cement for a second longer than necessary, so I asked the local coroner to pick his body up the second homicide released it."

"So, let's go," said Thomas.

"Jim," Hope said, "if the crime scene is still protected, I would like to go directly there. Is it anywhere near the police station, and, if so, could you guys drop me off? If it's out of the way, maybe I could take one of the cars we have here, if that's okay. I have a brand-new 'forensics' kit that Doctor Scott put together for me as a departure gift. I can scan the scene for forensics if the area has been protected. I would love to begin my day there. I'm super pumped to find that bastard who took Clint away from you, Jim, and from all of PIU."

What Hope didn't say, but made a note to ask her dad when they were alone, was 'shouldn't Jim have withdrawn from the case to be replaced by someone on the local police force?' She believed he was too close to the case, given that Clint was his partner.

Jim looked impressed. "Let me make a quick call."

He was having trouble holding back tears, so gave himself a minute or two to turn his back, while he was placing the call, to wipe them away.

After he ended the call, he turned back to them. "Good news, Hope. The crime scene will remain protected until you are able to view it. The homicide team doesn't have a problem with that request."

He seemed to be deep in thought, but not for long. "Thomas, why don't I call the station and let the team know that we are going to the crime scene first, and then we will come to them. It might be helpful for you to see it, too."

"Thank you, Jim." Hope was using her inside voice, and in the moment, Jim was okay with that. "Assuming that Clint's body has already been transferred to the morgue, if the autopsy has not been performed, I will ask permission to observe."

Jim nodded his approval.

43: Roger that

Paradise was set to return to Cape St Mary solo. After a lengthy and over-the-top breakfast with Sydney, her girl, Penelope, and her friend, Gary Langille, she was anxious to get on the road. She had a million questions about Sydney's relationship with Gary but that was for another day. This conversation might stretch out over a couple of days.

As she hugged Sydney while saying goodbye, Paradise whispered, "You're not fooling me. That man is more than a friend. We must plan a day to talk 'relationships' because I can answer your questions, and you must have a million of them. In fact, let's plan a two-day spa outing somewhere. What do you think? I'll find one and send you some information."

Sydney was silent for a second or two. Then she gave Paradise a big smile as she said, "Soon, please. I have never stepped inside of a spa, but I would love to have that experience with you. I *do not want* anyone putting cucumber slices to cover my eyes, though, so make sure you tell them that when you make our reservations."

"Oh, Sydney, we will have a great time. I'll be in touch with details very soon."

Paradise was halfway out the door, but Sydney followed her. "Paradise, what would you think of us bringing our girls with us?"

Paradise got in her car and turned the engine on. Only then did she roll down the window and respond. "*No.* We have years to take our girls to a spa. Understand that I will prepare a tutorial on relationships, and there will be pictures. Our girls already know all they need to know about sex, and I don't want them making fun of my 'stick man and stick women lets-have-sex,' figures. I see I've made you laugh, Sydney. My job here is done."

Sydney waved until Paradise backed out of the driveway, safely turned left, and disappeared. Once Paradise was on the highway and headed for home, she admitted to being depressed and lonely, too. Her husband was off working on a murder case in Ontario, along with her daughter. Her son, Lee was, she hoped, nearing the end of Grade 10 in Hawaii. Paradise made a mental note to touch base with Lee as soon as she arrived home for an update on when he intended to arrive. She knew his uncles would have to book a flight. Paradise and Thomas had offered to pay for Lee's airline ticket but since Lee had called several days ago, he and his uncles had gone silent.

Paradise always travelled with her relatively-new cell phone. Some days she even turned it on, and today was one of those days! With her family helter-skelter she wanted to be available to them one hundred percent of the time.

A couple of hours into her drive she stopped to stretch her legs, and while she walked around, she called Eugenie. Wilmot was keeping an eye on Eugenie, at least until Paradise got home, so she might not be alone. Paradise kept this in mind as she heard Eugenie's phone ring.

"Hello?"

"Hi, Eugenie, it's Paradise. How are you, my dear? You've been on my mind every second of every hour."

"I'm doing okay, Paradise, but I'm getting pretty fatigued, to be honest. Marie and Wilmot have been with me in shifts, so they are rested and relaxed, I think. I shouldn't be speaking for them, though. I told them to 'take it outside' while I answered my phone. They had a couple of friends drop in, so they brought them over."

Eugenie lowered her voice, even though everyone else was outside. "Do kids these days even have an 'inside voice'? Paradise, can you give me an example of when they should use it? I must have asked them to 'tone it down' a hundred times and they do...for an instant."

"I can ask Wilmot to send everyone home. If you like, I can kick both him and Marie out of your house right now. That would give you a few hours of peace and quiet before I check in..."

Paradise could tell by the soft sounds that Eugenie was making that she had something to say, perhaps she needed a night with no one else who was sleeping over…just her and her Pops, always.

"Paradise, you are always so kind and I don't know how to say this without offending you, but I would really appreciate an empty house tonight. I need the quiet so I can think of Pops and all that happened. It's all happened so fast. I know Wilmot and Marie are staying with me until you get home, so can I ask you to drop in and then after a bit of time take everyone out with you?"

Paradise felt there way more coming, so she remained silent.

"Remember my background. I was a nun for many years. My devoted love was for my God and together we looked after many individuals who were dying and came to us for that end-of-life period. My love for Pops was and is a totally different kind of love. I deal with grief in my own way, perhaps the opposite to how you grieve. Pops is in heaven. When someone dies, their soul is off to heaven instantly. I grieve with Pops every night when I go to sleep. Does any of this happen with you…when a loved one dies, I mean?"

Paradise thought for a moment. "My dear friend, having Wilmot and Marie with you was intended to make you feel safe and to remind you that you are not alone. It sounds to me like they have reminded you very loudly and repeatedly. Has it only been a couple days since Pops passed away? So much has happened since then. I have a suggestion for you. Ask everyone other than Wilmot and Marie to leave because you have some personal business to discuss with your 'chaperones' and you need to be alone with them. Trust me, they have a story that will last until I arrive. Tell them I have set this up to keep your mind occupied for a bit."

"That might work," Eugenie replied. "Be safe on the road, Paradise, please. Play some music or sing or something. Don't think about Pops' death, please. My home is full of all kinds of thoughts about death, so there will be ample time for you to grieve his passing tomorrow and in the days that follow."

Paradise thought she would sign off with Pops' signature. "Roger that."

Using her inside voice Eugenie asked, "I have told Pops a million times *I do not* understand that silly expression."

Paradise couldn't stop herself from laughing out loud.

The voice in her phone said, "Paradise, do you know the meaning behind the expression, 'Roger that'? If you do know the story, tell me *please.* Who is Roger? And what is 'that'?"

44: Soul stories

Wilmot was hesitant to share their past lives. "Eugenie, I'm not sure our story is one to share when there is such sorrow all around. Paradise was wrong to suggest that you ask us to outline our lives during and after the tragic time we survived. The 'Meat Loaf era', as the gang members proudly called it, was nothing short of murderous."

Wilmot looked to Marie for support. Her facial expression always gave her away, and this was no exception. Wilmot knew there would be strong support for Paradise and her request. He remained silent for the moment and was curious to hear how Marie would begin. How far back in their history would she go? She did not disappoint.

"Wilmot, it's true our story is both horrific and graphic, however we are here and alive to tell it. In this moment, the death of everyone's beloved Pops is, of course, all we can think of. Eugenie, you have such compassion for others I feel Paradise was right in asking that we share our story to keep your mind totally occupied. Wilmot, we will leave out the mushy part about how we met and fell in love, so I will begin, and if you want to take over at any time, feel free to do so."

She looked to Wilmot for his approval and got it in his smile and his, 'the floor is yours' hand gesture.

"Thank you, honey. Eugenie, Wilmot and I both worked for a company that, we would later learn, was a front for a mob. The head of that mob was my boss, Meat Cove. As a youth he grew up in Meat Cove, on Cape Breton Island, Nova Scotia, and when he started his own 'business' he moved to Ontario and took his village name as his own. No one knew why and no one asked. You only spoke when Meat spoke first.

"I did all the clerical work for him and his 'gang,' but never once did he explain what I was logging. It was always 'YH' or 'TH' or 'XZ' and every other combination of letters. I once asked him where the money really came from and where it went. That's when he started to abuse me.

"That first day he hit me so hard across the face that I fell to the floor. Next, he kicked me in the chest. I will never forget what he said to me. It hurt more than the slap or the kick."

Wilmot brought Marie a drink of water and asked if she was okay. Her response answered his question.

"Meat shouted at me, saying, 'Don't you ever ask me what goes on in my business, you got that? You do what I tell you to do and nothing else. Stupid cow. How dare you ask me *any* questions. Next time you step out of line I'll put my own gun in your mouth and shoot your face off.'

"Eugenie, I had been threatened at gunpoint by this despicable man too many times to be concerned. If he ever had to train someone else, God knows what he would do to them if they dared to ask a question."

Eugenie was on her feet, "I can't stand any more of this story, kids...unless you can skip to the end and tell me how it happens that you are here with us today and healthy enough to walk that cute dog of yours from end to end of Mavillette Beach seven days a week without fail. Some days, twice I believe."

Wilmot regained the floor. "I'll take it from here, honey, and I won't be long wrapping it up. Our last day with Meat Cove almost killed both of us. While one was beating me to death, another went to our home to do the same to Marie. I made it home to her, called for an ambulance and disappeared when I saw the flashing lights. I knew they would take care of her, and I was certain if I made it to the nearest ditch I would just lay down and die. I felt that I was that close to the end of my life.

"Somehow, and I may never know how, I woke up in a private clinic in Acapulco, Mexico, under the treatment of Doctor Gene Pat Bisogno, who brought me back from death's door, fixed my many broken bones and monitored my mental health. Because I had crawled home to Marie on badly broken bones, Doctor Bisogno was not able to save my lower legs. Today I walk okay, as you can see, and I can even walk on the beach. I couldn't do that at first because my balance was not great on uneven surfaces. Now, we walk on the beach so much that I require new prosthetics every other year.

"I am grateful for everything and everyone in my life today. I feel blessed to live here in the Cape in the company of family and such wonderful friends. And, if I may, just a touch of humour at my sister's expense. Of all the surprises this journey has brought me up to this very day, the biggest surprise of all came my way the day I called home and spoke with mom and dad. Give me a second or two to recall as accurately as I can."

"And what's up with my sister? How many years has she been in the convent now? I've kind of lost track of time."

"Oh, my son, you have so much to catch up on, and your sister is at the top of the list. Paradise left the convent and came here and lived with us."

Wilmot said, "Could I speak with her for a minute?"

"My goodness, son, she isn't here any longer. Paradise can fill in the blanks for you, but after learning she was adopted, she relocated to a very small village in Nova Scotia called Cape St Mary, where she learned what she needed to know, and much more. All from a man named Pops."

"Is that where I would have to go to find my sister? And why didn't I know she was adopted?"

Wilmot's mother said, "Your sister is a private investigator, working with a man named Thomas in Hawaii. Paradise was pregnant when she entered the convent. Somehow Thomas learned of this and was able to reunite her with her little girl, Hope—that's the name Paradise gave her. My son, there is so much more...all in good time."

Eugenie's heart was full of love for this family. "Now, that's a beautiful ending to the beginning of your new life. Thank you for sharing such personal information with me, Wilmot."

She turned to Marie as if to say, 'your turn'.

"Eugenie, would you like to hear how I came to be here today?"

"In the name of the lord, *yes!*" Eugenie clapped her hands as she spoke. "But not too sad and, I hope, no deaths."

"Good. I like to have equal time," Marie said. "There are many blanks in my story and that's because of the state I was in when I was taken to a hospital specializing in total healing. Meaning both physical and mental healing. I would learn many months later that the paramedics and doctors at the hospital I was first taken to felt mine was a revenge beating, meaning I would be unsafe as long as I stayed within the greater Toronto region. They whisked me away to a hospital with an adjoining rehab clinic several hours away from Toronto. The media was not told about the incident, and Meat would assume his men had killed me, so he looked no further.

"Eugenie, early in my hospitalization I could not move a finger. My physical injuries were not as traumatic as what Wilmot had to deal with. For me, it was my mental health that was shattered. I didn't know who I was, and I didn't know where I was. I didn't know what was wrong with me and I was afraid of anyone and everyone who came near me. I didn't have any rings on, so I assumed I wasn't married. I hated it when anyone came into my room because they would ask so many questions that I had no answers for.

"Did you sleep well, Marie?"

"Have you seen the sunshine we have today, Marie?"

"Are you ready for your physical therapy, Marie?'

"Are you ready for your mental health appointment, Marie?"

"Everyone on staff treated me as if they had no other patients to see that day.

"As I began to recover, the staff would cheer me on whenever they saw me. That was good for my ego, even though the cheer might have related to me combing my hair for the first time since being admitted. Baby steps.

"Wilmot eventually found me, and here we are. I go back annually for a full physical and mental health check-up. And, to be very honest, I like to return to those who put me back together so they can marvel at *their* work. There are always new employees, and the existing staff have their own way of taking credit for my recovery.

"Once, they asked me if I would mind if medical students accompanied the doctor for my appointment. I had no objection to this at all. They would talk as if I wasn't even in the room and the students were more interested in all the scans and MRI results up on the wall, so I basically saw the backside of everyone. The doctor would say something like, 'When this young woman arrived on our doorstep, she was in the worst shape we had ever seen. We put her back together physically and her rehab began. At that same time, we established a program related to the patient's mental health. This was the most difficult program for her. She never gave up. Not once. For example, the patient was hesitant to use the phone, to speak if anyone answered. She had to relearn how to communicate socially, and she would tell you that she hung up on more than a few calls we encouraged her to make. We had an inside joke with the patient about her making harassing phone calls.'"

Marie was quick to add, "I needed something to smile about and, while it was devastating for me to make a call repeatedly and hang up when the person answered, I saw it as a new beginning for me. I just had to suck it up and speak up."

"Marie, you have given me an idea," Wilmot said. "When I last saw Doctor Bisogno, he asked me to keep in touch and let him know if I found you and if we were both healthy and happy. I should write him a letter to give him some feedback, but what I would really like to do is ask him to visit us. I should have written as soon as I could make my fingers work again. Marie, would you help me put a letter together? You're better with words than I am."

"Absolutely!" Marie was beaming as she looked at her handsome husband.

"I second that," said Eugenie.

"Done. I am going to write that letter tomorrow. Doctor Bisogno will be so surprised to hear from me. He sat by my bedside and told me so many personal stories that I was convinced he thought I would die soon and that's why he was sharing so much with me."

"On that note," Eugenie spoke with excitement in her voice, "I see a car has just turned onto our road. I'm thinking this will be Paradise, so consider your assignment complete with an above-average grade. Thank you both for giving me a glimpse into your souls. You have given me an incredible gift that I will cherish. I do have one question, although I may regret asking it. Is this Meat Cove still out there ruining people's lives?"

"I'm glad you asked, Eugenie," Marie said, "because this is an important part of our history. Paradise drove to Port Hope (in her father's Cadillac I might add!) to speak with the PI partners there, Clint and Jim Taylor. With no warning at all someone started shooting through the front windows. All three PIs hit the floor and within seconds they were in place. Paradise was the one who first encountered the shooter, none other than Meat Cove. It was her that he was looking for. He was convinced she could lead him to Wilmot. I am happy and proud to share that Paradise, my sister the nun turned private investigator, shot and killed the bastard... deader than a door nail. Any questions, Eugenie? Would you like more detail about the shoot-out? I can brag about my bad-ass sister all day."

"I believe I have learned quite enough from the two of you today. Thank you and please stand down, as Pops liked to say."

45: An idea to share

Sydney and her daughter learned more and more about each other as every day passed. Sydney had been planning her return-to-work date, but more recently she began to consider retirement instead. Her financial advisors assured her that she had invested her money wisely and could retire today if she chose to. Sydney's mental health had required Doctor Gary Langille to step in.

He advised her to be certain she had one or two hobbies that she was passionate about before retiring. He didn't want her to have any time to think back to the day she was almost murdered. Getting to know Penelope would be an excellent hobby, if Sydney could remember to not smother her. Hope's departure and the way it all happened pained Sydney. She had deep regrets. She felt it all happened under a cloud of anger, on both sides.

It was not easy for Sydney and suddenly she truly needed to patch things up with young Hope. Only when Hope drove away did Sydney realize she had been a tutor and nothing more. In all those years, she had never thought of Hope as a friend. She had never treated Hope to a day off or even a dinner out after a hard day's work.

Sydney decided she would make a few calls and have a forensics kit put together for Hope. If she really wanted to work in forensic sciences, she needed to begin those studies.

Penelope didn't know of her mother's retirement plans, and that was deliberate. Sydney had been smothering Hope for years without realizing it and she vowed to herself to never, ever, make Penelope feel that way. Today might be the day she would share her ideas with her daughter.

She could hear Penelope walking along the hallway connecting her suite with the main house. They had developed an early-morning routine of having coffee together when they both continued to appear for that first cup before or just minutes after six am. It amazed Sydney how alike they were and yet, until recently they had never met. She didn't even own a photograph of her daughter.

"Good morning, mom." Penelope smiled as she took what had become her seat at the kitchen table for the early-morning coffee.

"Good morning, my sweet girl. Did you sleep well? I was worried when I finally began to doze off that I had gone on and on too much about the importance of your education as you move on in this world. I fell asleep with a not-too-distant memory of Hope shouting at me that she had had enough education shoved down her throat. I never want to make you feel that way." Sydney could see that Penelope had something on her mind.

"I, too, fell asleep with a not-too-distant memory: of giving up my apartment and moving into what they called a bed-sitting room in my hometown in the province of Quebec. Nowhere felt like home, so over the past decade I kept moving, still looking over my shoulder and still hoping to one day meet my birth mother. Since you asked, I did feel, for the first time since the day I met you, some pressure coming from you as we discussed what university I should attend next. Mother, I do have one degree already, as I have explained more than once. Initially I thought you had just forgotten about this milestone. You dismissed my Bachelor of Fine Arts like it's nothing at all. I had to scrimp and save to put myself through university and complete my first degree. I'm proud of that! Please, don't take that pride away from me."

Penelope took a breath, and a sip of coffee. "I apologize, mother. I'm trying, but sometimes anger pops up and I am only just learning how to manage it. I hope I haven't upset you at this early hour in the day."

"I'm trying, too, my dear. As God is my witness, I'm trying. I take every word you have spoken to heart, and I will not dismiss your accomplishments ever again. I can't begin to imagine the struggles you have faced from the very day you were born. Your determination and grit have brought you to my doorstep. You are the baby who was taken away from me the second you were born." Sydney found herself crying. "I *did not give you away, Penelope,* you were stolen from me, leaving me thinking I would never see you again. Yet here we are. Thank you, God."

Sydney could see that she had upset Penelope, and she knew why. Just after she arrived, she had asked her mother, 'why did you give me away?' That question took them through it all and when they had finished, they vowed to never bring that day up again. Everything that needed to be said had been said.

"Leaving that discussion filed away as we promised we would do, mother; can I refill our coffee cups? I want to share something totally different with you. Something I have not raised, but it's been on my mind since I was a young teenager bouncing from mother to mother, home to home and too often ending up in a shelter for 'runaway-teens.' That's the moniker beside my name on the cover of the file that seemed to follow me everywhere...except here. Today I am totally unburdened, thanks to you and to Paradise, and excited to share an idea with you. I need coffee, so it's your turn for a minute or more."

"How would you feel about taking a year off to travel around the world with me? I have never, and I'm ashamed to admit this, taken one day's vacation. Swear to God. I could retire anytime, and we would have more money than we could spend in our lifetimes, so that's not an issue. I hope this has sunk in by now: you never have to worry about money."

Sydney had no idea what Penelope wanted to discuss, but she wasn't ready to let her have the floor just yet. "Please, just think about my offer. If nothing comes of it, that will be okay. I've never had the urge to travel the world until you came into my life. Now I see the world differently. I have a reason to get out of bed each morning, and it's not because I'm anxious to get to my morgue."

Sydney sat back and laughed at herself. "Seems your mother is pretty dull, don't you think?"

"Mother, that's quite a leap from going to your offices to going around the world, don't you think? You might be feeling the need to get away from this house, but if I live to be 100, I will never take anything for granted. Quite the mansion you have here."

Sydney wasn't connecting the dots. "You said you have an idea you are excited to share with me. Your idea doesn't relate to my home specifically, I assume, so get to it kiddo. What do you have?"

Silence.

"Seriously, Penelope, please go on." Sydney was intrigued.

"Because I feel so fortunate today, right now, this very second, I am never going to look back," Penelope said. "I have been thinking of trying my luck at getting a job in the non-profit industry. I would like to help women and children in some way. Women and children who have fled an abusive relationship, for example. Or single women, like me, who have been kicked around their entire life and need some grounding and a bit of help to get back on their feet. Mom, if I need specific education or training to work in the industry, I'll get it. Halifax has at least a couple of shelters for women and some great programs, too. What we would build would be different. See how I worked 'we' in there? Wouldn't it be wonderful if we could launch a home like this...right in this house? We could turn your part of the mansion into that space, initially, and you and I could live in 'my quarters', which, in my opinion, is yet another mansion. I know we could get government grants, and we could fund-raise as well. We could ask businesswoman to select one of their office suits and donate it to us so we could help women who are getting on their feet again look as confident as they feel when they leave us and move on to opportunities. Does this interest you at all?"

Sydney said, "Don't get ahead of yourself with this idea, Penelope. I think it's a great idea, but baby steps. For example, let's not collect women's office suits before we put pen to paper. Costs. Viability. Sources from A to Z. Community needs. Etcetera. So, consider me 'all in', as Hope would say. I would be absolutely delighted to work on this project with you. However, do I sense that our world cruise is already off the table? Did my pitch fall flat?"

"Our cruise is not 'off the table', but it might be pushed to the very back of the table. I promise you; we will get to it one day. Honestly, mom, I'm feeling the need to earn my way, and going around the world right now won't accomplish that. Let's think about a compromise, though. What if we spent a month or two gathering all the facts and figures we need before we can sit down with an accounting firm, and then, *only then*, maybe we could go on a two-week cruise where we would work in the mornings but close the books for the rest of the day and evening. You could be my teacher in the mornings for those facts and figures I might not fully understand. In the afternoon I could be your teacher for those times you just can't stop working. We can learn to have fun together. I haven't had many happy moments in my life. Who am I kidding? I haven't had *any*, and, if you think back, perhaps you haven't had too many either. And that's all I have to say on the subject."

Sydney was smiling as she got up and went around the table to give her daughter a hug. A real mother-to-daughter hug. "It's official: you are in charge of 'fun' and I will willingly do whatever you say."

"Sounds great, Sydney, and let's make a promise to try very hard to not look back. God has brought us together for a reason."

"God may have had a hand in it, but I have personally paid private investigator Paradise d'Entremont over a full year's salary to make it happen, so could we agree that God pushed Paradise to you and you to me...so we have a chance to start over. As you say, no looking back."

"Roger that," Penelope replied. "I hear Hope saying that to her mother when they end a phone call. I liked it, so she said I could use it anytime I like."

"Roger that," Sydney said, smiling as she left the kitchen without looking back.

46: The gang's all here

Paradise visualized Eugenie, all alone, watching for her to come home. She could remember seeing both Eugenie and Pops many a time, sitting at the kitchen window. Their entertainment consisted of sitting in the window and trying to name every person who walked past their home. They knew everyone by name and, for the most part, they knew something about their lives, too.

She put her blinker on to indicate she would be turning left onto Pops and Eugenie's Road. It was a short road, but when Paradise opened her door to step out of her car, Eugenie was already outside and headed her way in her housecoat and slippers.

"As the Lord is my witness, Paradise, I am so happy to have you home. I would never admit this to Wilmot and Marie, but they were trying too hard to keep my mind off my husband and I'm sure I told them fifty times that it was better for me to talk about Pops… and to hear others praise Pops in their own way. I never got through to them, so I just shut up and hoped you were on your way. That's not a very nice 'welcome' home, dear. I'm sorry."

"Eugenie, let's get you back inside. It's cold out here this late in the evening. We need you healthy and strong for a long time. Understand? This is a personal question, and I apologize if I offend you, but exactly how many years younger than Pops are you? I was trying to figure that out as I was driving home, and I'm guessing it's more than twenty years, am I right?"

"Pops once told me he was born an old man, and he figured everyone was forever younger than him. Yes, I think I am a couple of decades younger than Pops. The very first day we spoke was at Café Central. The place was full. I was sitting alone at a table, and I saw Pops come in. He filled the entire doorway as he entered and my first thought was, 'That is one very big man, rugged and hand-some, too,' and don't you know he brought his coffee over to my table and asked if he could join me. Little did Pops know I had just arrived back home in Meteghan after decades in the convent. Now I am freezing Paradise, let's stop talking at least until we get inside. Oh, there might be one or two family members patiently waiting to give you a hug."

"Wait until I get my overnight bag out of the trunk. I am bunking in with you tonight, and that's not up for discussion. Must be Wilmot and Marie inside and we're keeping them waiting. And you are freezing cold, so go ahead of me, please."

"No! That's not the plan. I mean there isn't a plan, but go ahead of me, please."

As Paradise looked up after dropping her jacket and bag on the floor in the porch, she met a pair of familiar eyes. She hadn't seen those eyes in over ten years.

~

Lee had recently turned sixteen, and those eyes were in the face of a young man. Lanky, and arms and legs like the 'stick people' that he had played with as a small child.

"Hello, mother. I'm hoping you're happy to see me. You're more beautiful than in the photo I took of you just before we left for the airport, all those years ago. Please, say something."

He was suddenly afraid that coming home had been a mistake. His mother seemed to recognize him, but was glued to the floor at the same time. She wasn't even blinking.

Lee wished he hadn't asked his uncles to wait until they saw her car coming along Cape St Mary Road. He could use some support, and he didn't want to approach his mother for a hug until she said something. Anything.

"My son."

Paradise could hardly speak so, in true mother fashion, she simply spread her arms wide as a tear escaped and threatened to give her away. Lee took two long steps forward and into his mother's arms. His awkwardness almost knocked her down and Eugenie, who was right behind his mother, took the force of their meeting!

"In the name of the Lord, Lee," Eugenie said, "watch what you're doing. My God, boy, help me get up. Nothing is broken, I hope. I have too much to do for Pops' Celebration of Life. We don't know when it will be held, but I'm in charge of everything. Yes, Paradise, I will delegate things for you to complete."

Still hugging her son, Paradise replied, "Anything, Eugenie. I would do anything for Pops, and Thomas and our children feel the same way. You'll have the Celebration in our home, I hope? However, you may have already decided on another venue. Again, just ask. It's late now, but maybe over that all-important first cup of coffee tomorrow morning, we can make a list of all that needs to be done. How does that sound?"

"It sounds like you think I can't get a list started without you. Well, just you wait until it's morning and I present my list to you. Together we will make it *our* list, but that's only once you contribute something that I haven't already thought of. I can already check one thing off: asking if we can have the Celebration in your home. Thanks, Paradise. That means a lot to me and, on that note, I will give both of you some privacy because I'm off to bed. Good night."

"Good night, Granny," said Lee.

His mother followed with, "Night night, Eugenie and quickly, close your bedroom door or you will never get to bed...we've got company. I hear heavy steps on the porch."

Turning to her son, Paradise said, "Lee, is this who I think it is joining us?"

She opened the door to the mudroom and, sure enough, there they were. Larger than life! Denis and Waine, Lee's uncles from Honolulu.

"Is it okay that we drop in like this, Paradise? We tried to give you some time alone with Lee, but we decided we didn't want to miss the celebration." Denis paused before going on. "We are so sorry for your loss. Every corner of the Cape is in mourning. Not surprising given how loved Pops was by everyone. Poor Eugenie is gutted."

Paradise gave Denis a big hug and moved him in out of the mud room so she could give Waine a hug, too. "It is so wonderful to see you, Waine. Can I ask how you are… your mental health, I mean."

Waine had always thanked Paradise for asking about his mental health and treating it as such a normal part of his health in general. "Follow me to the party, Waine."

Taking Waine by the hand, Paradise brought him into the kitchen as she shouted, "Hail, hail, the gang's all here!"

"Mother," Lee said, "I remember so vividly, and I was five at the time, how whenever you answered the door to greet someone it seemed an hour went by before you brought whoever it was into the rest of the house. As evidenced by how bloody long you took to get these two into the kitchen. The party's almost over, because I'm falling asleep."

He put his arm around his mother, so naturally. "Mom, we arrived late yesterday so all we did today was buy a few groceries for #3. I'll stay with my uncles for as many nights as you are here with Eugenie. She needs you now. I get that. I'll have you all to myself soon enough. Are Dad and Hope arriving tomorrow? What is everyone doing that you're all away somewhere other than home, by the way?"

"My son, let's call it a night. I know you have a million questions, and I'll answer every single one of them, I promise. I hope to only stay with Eugenie for one night, and I plan to bring her to our place for a few nights, but you and I will have some alone time soon."

Party over. Everyone to bed. Tomorrow would be another day.

47: Guns drawn

In Port Hope, while Thomas and a homicide detective sat with the parents of the young victim, the local police force was narrowing in on the second suspect.

Nothing would bring their son back but if the parents could help the police find who murdered their only child, their home was open to them. They felt responsible for Clint's murder and kept asking if they could meet with Jim.

Thomas was honest in his response. "Jim is grieving and in no shape to meet with anyone. He is totally broken, and I'm worried about him."

They understood.

"I promise you this," Thomas added. "We will keep you informed as this case moves forward and I will personally let you know when my daughter, Hope, and I are leaving town and what Jim's plans are, if he is able to make any decisions in the short term. So don't feel that we will abandon you...we will not rest until the second shooter is caught and brought to justice. You have my word."

Meanwhile, back at the PIU building, Hope wanted to keep Jim's mind occupied and decided to offer to teach him a few things about the world of forensics.

"I am puzzled by one thing. You came to the crime scene with a totally modern forensics kit. Am I correct in thinking this morning was the first time you have used it? How did you put all of that to-gether in record time? And how did you even know what to equip a forensics kit with?"

"The credit goes to my mentor in Halifax, Doctor Scott. Not to say she compiled this array of tools all herself. This woman 'knows people' and they adore her, and are happy to make things happen for her." Jim shared that the local police had informed him that the body found nearby was wearing a ski mask, so the assumption could be made that his partner did, too. They had seen the photo of the man who had murdered a young teenager simply because he was gay. "Do you know what I hope? I hope that the one shot I took, killed the bastard who snuffed out a life with nothing but a clean slate ahead of him."

He shook his head. "Hope, I need to talk about something else for a little while until my heart settles down so I'm going to ask you to do me a favour. I watched you as we approached the crime scene, and you were totally zoned in. Can you tell me what your thoughts were as you circled the scene? Do you already have forensic training?"

"I don't know a lot of forensic stuff yet," Hope said, "and it's true that today I visited my first crime scene. As a result, I know more about my new-found profession than I did yesterday and that has to count for something."

"I'm with you all the way, kid. Move on with educating me about forensics, though. Teach me something."

"Jim, I'm about to share specific learnings Sydney has given me but I want to preface the details by saying that I have spoken with a few private investigators with a specific interest in forensics, and everyone has said the same thing. Forensics, and forensic pathology in particular, takes you places you didn't know you were not equipped to delve into. Initially you think you're fine to go there, but what if you're not capable of coming back? It does happen, apparently, but in all honesty, I have not been around long enough to state that with any authority. Let's hope I'm not the one who can't come back!"

Hope was only partially kidding. For just an instant she doubted her ability to grasp the world of forensics.

"Sydney and I had just begun my forensics education. She felt she needed a refresher so we could learn together. I don't think that was true. The woman is a human library. She also thought I should continue my 'proper' education until I qualified to become a medical examiner. I would be old and grey if I had to stay in school for that many years. I will begin by sharing some data that Sydney made interesting with things like 'The 7 Ss of Crime Scene Investigation.'

1. Secure the scene
2. Separate all witnesses
3. Scan the full scene
4. See the scene (different from securing the scene)
5. Sketch the scene
6. Search for evidence
7. Secure and collect evidence

Hope paused to pull her notebook from her backpack. Jim made himself useful with a fast trip to the kitchen to find a soft drink for each of them.

"Jim, I assume these 7 Ss apply to your work as well. A trained PI and a trained forensic PI would both begin with the above. As you observed, I have the 7 Ss memorized. Memorizing stuff is my thing. But to continue I need my notes."

She flipped to the page she wanted. "Next, we move on to a successful *forensic* investigation." She interrupted herself and looked up. "The day I mentioned my interest in forensic investigations to Sydney, in the blink of an eye she had me preparing to study at a top-notch university anywhere in the world. That's the night I packed up and drove to Cape St Mary and my home."

Jim said, "You're quite a success for a 22-year-old. Do I have your age correct?

"Very flattering so thank you. You're off by three digits. Now, can I keep teaching you about forensics or do you need a break? It does get heavy going forward, so if you've had enough just say the word."

"Hope, let's split up, if you don't mind. I need some alone time to grieve my loss."

He was barely holding it together and Hope was sorry she hadn't seen that earlier. "Me as well. I need a bit of time to grieve

Pops' death, and to see if I can reach my mom. She's in the Cape by now. From my room upstairs I can see the driveway, so if I see headlights turning in, we will know it's my dad and I will be down those stairs two or three at a time. Is that okay with you?"

"Let's put a time on it, though. If your dad returns past 2 am, we owe it to him to allow time for him to sleep. He will wake us up if he needs to talk to us before the morning. It's 12:30 am now, Hope, so get yourself in bed so you can, at the very least, close your eyes."

Five minutes later Hope came running back down the stairs.

"Jim I've got your next lesson in PI forensics, taught by yours truly," she said. "Well, *printed* by yours truly is more like it. I didn't mention this lesson until I was able to check some computer files on my laptop. If you can't sleep you could read this document while you wait for my dad to reappear."

"Hope, you're beginning to sound like a clone of your Doctor Sydney Scott. Be careful you aren't all work and no play, as the saying goes. I am sure this will put me to sleep at some point, so thanks for the printed lesson."

"Message received," said Hope. She disappeared upstairs as Jim began reading…

The scientific method

Step one: Recognize the need (observe)
After a professional or casualty event occurs, the first step is to identify the problem. Forensic experts must determine the root cause and origin of the incident and assign responsibility. Identifying the cause and responsible party helps prevent similar incidents from reoccurring in the future.

Step two: Define the problem (question)
An action plan is developed to solve the problem. This plan outlines a strategic, step-by-step investigation aimed at addressing the issue.

Step three: Collect data (research)
Forensic experts conduct a preliminary visit or inspection of the site where the incident occurred and gather evidence. It is crucial to collect all available data associated with the incident scene before analyzing or hypothesizing, ensuring the development of an unbiased hypothesis free from speculation.

Step four: Analyze the data (hypothesize)
This step involves a thorough analysis of all collected data. Experts in relevant fields may be consulted to provide their specialized knowledge.

Step five: Develop the hypothesis (experiment)
Based on the data analysis results, as well as the professionals' expertise, education and training, forensic investigators develop potential hypotheses. Multiple hypotheses are commonly considered at this stage.

Step six: Test the hypotheses (analyze)
Each hypothesis is tested against all known facts and evidence. This may involve physical testing to gather additional data that supports or refutes the hypotheses. Any hypothesis not supported by the evidence must be discarded. Hypothesis testing is a strict and repetitive process that concludes when all feasible hypotheses have been tested, and those disproven have been eliminated.

Step seven: Select the hypothesis (conclude)
After evaluating, testing and rejecting multiple hypotheses, only one hypothesis will remain that cannot be ruled out. This final hypothesis identifies the root cause of the event.

Step eight: Share findings with the client (communicate)
For client-facing forensic experts, an additional step is crucial. Forensic investigations and analyses involve complex

findings and highly technical information that may be difficult for the average person to understand. However, clients have a common need to comprehend the issue and gain their own perspectives on the incident to make informed decisions. The ability to communicate complex findings in plain language is vital. Forensic investigators act as translators, conveying complex information in a manner easily understood by insurance company professionals.

Several hours later, Jim called out for Hope to get out of bed and downstairs fast. "Thomas will want to debrief with both of us present. Hope, are you awake?"

Hope made it downstairs before her father got out of the car. Both she and Jim could see that Thomas was hurting. He kept his hand on the vehicle for balance as he took a few steps before Jim and Hope were out the door, saying, "How can we help? Should you lean on us dad?" Hope was in tears.

"Just get me inside and, Jim, I'll need a very cold beer." Thomas was pressing his hand against his left side.

"You got it, boss, but I have to raise something that needs to be addressed." Jim was nervous and tried to lighten the moment. "Hope, when we are all at work, you need to call your father 'Thomas', not 'Dad.' It's hard to explain but this could be a safety issue. One of us, or others we might work with, the local police here for example, might blink hearing 'dad' or think dad is a code name for a project."

"Got it. Now let's get *Thomas* inside."

48: A trail of staples

Thomas spoke in a whisper. "It's over, Jim."

He reached out to take a second beer. He had guzzled the first as he stood in a hot shower, having promised Jim and Hope he would be of greater value to any discussion if he cleaned up first. Thomas knew they had seen the blood on his clothes, and a shower gave him the opportunity to reappear in a less-shocking way...in this case he opted for pj's.

"It was a clean shot, Jim. It's over. You shot the murderer, but because you rushed to Clint's side you didn't think about removing his mask to see who he was. Just know the bullet that killed the bastard came from your gun.

"The parents of the young man, whom he murdered solely because he was gay, had only just 'come out' to his parents. Because of this, they wanted to help in any way they could. They pored over literally hundreds of photos of their son's friends at different stages of their young lives and, from a picture at the bottom of the storage bin that held so many memories—mostly happy stories that included their son—they identified the best friend of the man you killed.

"He was a predator who made his living by grabbing gay men and women off the street, in their homes, in bars, even in their place of worship. After using them for his own pleasure, one by one he 'sold' them to the highest bidder. For cash in hand he would, without so much as a sober second thought, put a bullet in someone's head. He treated these souls like trash."

"Thomas," Hope began, quite proud of herself at this time of the early morning that she didn't forget and call him *dad*. "When you say that this couple identified the best friend of the man that Jim had already killed, are you saying this is the man *you* shot?"

"That's right, sweetheart—I mean daughter of mine...I mean Hope. Now, about the blood you saw on my clothes—"

Hope said, "Spill, Thomas. Tell us everything and then we will let you go to bed and sleep as long as you need. The sun is coming up so...talk fast!"

"Hope, one thing you will learn quickly in this business is that it's imperative you compartmentalize thoughts that you take away at the end of every assignment. It's a job in itself to not let one case be blurred by the next one. Long after each case, you may be called on to revisit it, and that's when you take the case out of that corner of your mind where you had tucked it away. You will be amazed how much your brain retains and can call up—"

"Dad, for the love of God tell us about *this* job. You can 'train me' on whatever you want another time. Talk us through the hunt and the kill, *please.*"

Jim added, "Begin with the blood, Thomas. Were you shot? Should we take you to the hospital? How are you feeling right now?"

Thomas didn't want to appear angry, but he couldn't help it. He *was* angry. "I attempted to explain the blood on my clothes when I arrived. I will do that now if you will both be quiet. The local homicide team took the case almost instantly once Clint had been murdered. The courtesy they have shown by allowing us to shadow someone from the homicide squad is huge. Homicide has been tracking both men for over a year. They have left a trail of 'kills' throughout the province and only when Clint was murdered were they able to connect the dots."

He shook his head. "All eight of the individuals who were executed were part of the gay community. Homicide's data collection confirmed that not all had come out to their families and close friends, so we will not announce any connection to the gay community. With this second kill, and again, Jim, the first kill goes to you, the leaders of the pack are both deceased."

He stretched out his leg gingerly. "My left leg was hit in the crossfire. I've got a mean trail of staples that they will remove in seven days. Hope, we will stick around until then. I am to keep my leg elevated for a couple of days, and no running, of course."

Thomas watched all colour leave Hope and Jim's faces. He could see that both had questions. Most likely lots of questions. Holding his hands up, he continued. "I have been prescribed heavy pain killers. I need to take one almost as much as I need to sleep. And I promise to answer all outstanding questions over early morning coffee."

Hope gently hugged her father. "Dad, I'm going to run upstairs and create that level of elevation you will need in your bed. I love you so much and I'm very proud of you."

With that, she hurried out of the room. Her tears were her own. From the top of the stairs, she called, "Dad, I will let you make that first call home. I promised mother we would contact her as soon as you arrived."

"Already done, Hope. I called Paradise as I was being stapled at the hospital. And forget the elevation in my bed. I can't climb the stairs, so for the next few days I'm taking Jim's room, and he will be in mine. *Good night, Hope!*"

Within minutes three private investigators were sleeping soundly.

49: Reporting in

Thomas called home from Jim's bed as soon as he woke up."Good morning, Thomas." Paradise said. "I am assuming this is you calling to apologize for falling asleep on our call last night, even though I dropped my negligee to the floor to keep you awake at least until you finished telling me about your injury."

She was smiling, but was also beyond worried about her husband. He had sounded like a ghost when he called in the middle of the night. He had no idea what time it was, and Paradise wondered if he might have been in a state of shock. He seemed totally confused and she wanted to get some answers during their call, and then all she heard was light snoring.

She had sat up all night beside the bloody telephone, which was in the most inconvenient spot in the house. They had renovations coming up, and Paradise would make sure to have a few more 'jacks' installed.

"That cannot be true, can it? I never miss one of your sex shows." Whenever Paradise undressed in front of him, and she did that almost every night, he had always had the same comment: 'Let the sex show begin!' "Start from where you nodded off, please. You were sitting in a bed with a couple of homicide detectives protecting you. Talk to me, my love."

"The detectives took the case, with the local force as back up, the night Clint was killed. Their file was titled 'homophobic kill with intent.' When I met up with them, they already had a hit on who the second shooter was, and knew where their gang was going to be. They called themselves, all in one word, 'gaysBgone', and they were incredibly proud of their logo. They wore the badge proudly on the shoulder of their black leather jackets. We waited until they came out of their clubhouse and dispersed to their individual black cars. Two were sharing a ride, one being the partner of the thug who murdered Clint, and that car was the last to leave. We could see that they were armed, and we suspected they wore more than one gun."

There was a pause, and Paradise could tell Thomas was taking a sip of water.

Then he continued, "We were out of our car, while they seemed content to sit in their car, talking and going nowhere. Trying for the element of surprise we crept to the back of their car and made a dash for each of the car doors, pointed our guns and shouted, 'Out of the car with your hands in the air.' They responded immediately by slamming their car doors open with such force that we were off balance...for less than a second, but that's all it took. It was the worst 'kill' I have ever been involved in. In a nutshell, Paradise, they were both killed, but not before killing a member of the local police force and shooting me in the thigh, right into the large muscle. I don't recall at what stage I called you from the hospital, but I was hyped up on pain medication. The hospital was crazy busy, but they looked after me immediately. Wait until you see my staples. The two men waiting for me when I was brought back to my room were with me in the gunfight. They had the sad task of telling me one of their own had died in the exchange. Dead at thirty years of age, leaving his wife and newborn twins."

"Thomas, maybe you should stop there. You've been talking a long time, which is very unlike you. Save the rest for our next call. And, as I sit here sipping my first cup of coffee, I suspect you haven't had your first cup yet, have you?"

"A woman who knows me well. I can smell the coffee brewing, and I can hear Hope and Jim speaking as quietly as they can. I would pass you over to our daughter, but she won't want to miss the rest of our debriefing that began when I got in last night, so I'll have her call you after breakfast. I want to hear about the funeral for Pops and how Eugenie is doing, and have you heard from Lee and...well...our life in general. Maybe you can discuss all of that with Hope and I will call you later this afternoon."

"Sounds good. Bye for now, my love. Give my love to Hope and Jim and tell them that my heart is with all of you."

50: An early appointment or two

Eugenie was disappointed with Paradise, and she would tell her so. The understanding was that Paradise would join Lee and his uncles over an hour ago to brainstorm with Eugenie about how best to remember Pops. Lee was anxious to move home rather than stay with the uncles for another day. They talked about it late last night and Paradise had promised Lee she would join everyone at Eugenie's early this morning.

It was already 8 am and Eugenie had fed the masses and was getting tired of keeping the coffee warm for Paradise. There was no excuse for her not showing up as she had promised.

Plus, Eugenie had a funeral to plan and had hoped for some assistance from Paradise. Yes, Eugenie was going to give Paradise an earful the second she showed up. She wouldn't have been late if Pops was alive! Losing Pops gave Eugenie the first and the worst heartache she had ever experienced.

Paradise entered the kitchen in a flurry and Eugenie lit into her before even looking her way. "Paradise d'Entremont, what is going on with you? Did you forget your son had plans to meet you here for breakfast over an hour ago? I am just about at wits' end, and I was counting on you today."

As Eugenie slapped a mug in front of Paradise, she finally looked at her while she poured her coffee.

Lee interrupted, "Mom, what's wrong? You look like you've been crying all night, and you have the same clothes on that you wore yesterday."

Even choosing them carefully, it was difficult for Paradise to say the words. "Son, your father is going to be okay, but he was involved in a shoot-out last night. He called me in the middle of the night, literally fell asleep while he was trying to fill me in, so you're right, Lee, I have not been sleeping. I was ready to leave the house to join you all this morning when he called again."

"Was he hurt," Lee asked.

"He will be fine. Son, your dad was shot in his right leg, in the muscle and fat surrounding his thighbone. I will leave that for you to discuss the details with your dad...assuming you want to. The bullet stopped a hairsbreadth before it would have shattered his femur. The surgeon said he had never seen a bullet lodged that way."

Pausing to reach out for Eugenie's hand Paradise continued, "I'm thinking Pops got his angel wings and saw what was happening. He wasn't 'trained' to use his wings so was late to the party. However, he arrived in time to alter the trajectory of the bullet. Thomas can't fly until he is healed enough to travel and the staples are removed. It will be about a week."

Turning her attention to Eugenie, Paradise said, "Never in a million years would I have expected you to judge me this way. Even before I had a chance to explain. Have I ever been an hour late to join you? *Ever?*"

"*Jesus, Mary and Joseph,* I swear, Paradise, I don't know what possessed me this morning. My nerves are shot, I'm not looking forward to planning the funeral. Can you ever forgive me? I also missed a doctor's appointment at 7:45 this morning. I desperately need something for my nerves, and for depression, too. The worst part is Pops would be disappointed with me."

On cue the uncles, who had been listening from the next room, appeared. "Let's go, Eugenie," Waine said. "We are going to drive you to the doctor's office, and we will bring you home as well. Please let us do this little thing for you."

"All is forgiven, Eugenie, and I'm sure you understand why I couldn't cut my call with Thomas short this morning. You would have had no way of knowing why I was not at your door when I said I would be."

51: The next day

With Lee, Eugenie, Waine and Denis on her team, Paradise was on a mission to bring the Cape family together...by this evening. They might be over-reaching, but were committed to trying.

"My God, Mom, what time did you get up this morning?" Lee thought 8 am was early enough, but apparently not when there were things to do.

He noticed several lists on the kitchen table. Under his name there was only one thing. He thought he would let his mother explain this, because it made no sense to him.

He reached for the coffee pot and a freshly made chocolate chip muffin. His mother had gotten to the coffee pot before he did, and had coffee brewing for the masses.

It was good to be with his mother, Lee thought. Everything she did seemed to flow towards her next move. He could learn so much from her and, even though he was learning a ton from his uncles, there was something much more personal about learning from your mom.

Lee's birth mother, Wikolia, passed away before he had time to learn from her or create memories with her. So as a young lad, he began to bond with Paradise...who was truly his mother in every way except one.

She emerged, freshly showered and dressed, and witnessed the look of confusion on her son's face. "Good morning, my son. May I begin with 'language' and remind you not to use the name of the Lord in any way other than in showing respect to the Lord, or when you are speaking to him: 'my Lord' or 'my God'."

"Duly noted," replied Lee with a smile. "Mom, your use of the word 'language' to correct any of us is something that I remember from before I left the Cape at a very young age. Where do I begin my job for the day? I might need a bit more 'training' than the one line you wrote."

"The first thing you need to do is call your dad in Port Hope. I told him that you are home for a few months, and he asked that you call him when you get up. If I pour you a hot cup of coffee, assuming that's what you were reaching for, you could go into the living room and take over the window seat. Your sister does that all the time. It's comfortable for all of us...but you just might be too tall to enjoy it. Here's your coffee...off you go. I can easily keep busy here at the kitchen table, so this is where you will find me."

~

Paradise passed a coffee to Lee and shooed him away. She had promised to call her brother early this morning so they could activate their plan.

"Paradise, is that you?" Wilmot answered the phone on one ring. "Marie is right beside me, sis, so tell us where to begin. I've no doubt you have things planned out already."

Marie added, "Paradise, we will do anything you want us to do. No job is too small. Maybe some will be too big but, if so, we will talk with you about it."

Paradise could hear her smile.

"If you are ready now, please pick Eugenie up and bring her here. I've got breakfast on the go for everyone. I don't want anything to upset Eugenie as I did when I arrived at her door much later than planned yesterday morning. We made up as soon as she understood why I was late. One of you could call her and tell her you are on your way over. That will allow her a minute or two to fetch her coat, her ever-growing list of things to do in honouring Pops, and the medication that her doctor gave her just yesterday for anxiety and depression. Please ensure she has her medication when she gets into your car. I want to help her remember to take it as prescribed."

Wilmot said, "Should we stop at cabin #3 and make sure the big guys are awake?"

"Not necessary. The uncles are already out on a mission for me. They have a number of things to do."

The call ended with everyone off and doing what needed to be done.

Paradise could hear Lee still on the phone with his dad. This made her happy. It had been a decade since father spoke to son. The content of their discussion would be difficult to have with any young man, but Lee seemed so grown up and ready to help his family, so she was moving forward with his list based on that.

Within minutes of her call to Wilmot, Paradise opened her door to Eugenie, Wilmot and Marie. "Come in, please. Coffee is hot and the pancakes are ready. I've made way too many, so you will have to eat plenty!"

Eugenie spotted Lee immediately. "Isn't it kind of early for Lee to be on the phone? Kids these days simply do not respect us at—"

Paradise felt she needed to have a wellness check with Eugenie and that interrupting her tirade was necessary. "Eugenie, Lee has been speaking with his father, and I believe he is now saying 'hi' to his sister. It's been over a decade since Lee has spoken with either. During my call with Thomas, the call that made me late and made you so angry with me, I shared that his son had come home. We promised that father and son, and then Lee and Hope, would talk early this morning."

Putting her arm around Eugenie, Paradise lowered her voice as she said, "I know you have medication to help you stay a bit calmer than you are at this moment. Have you taken your meds this morning?"

When Eugenie began to cry and shake her head 'no' Paradise took her by the hand, and they disappeared into the washroom together.

As soon as the women returned to the table, Lee wanted to get busy working through the list he saw on the counter by a coffee that surely belonged to Paradise. Once his mother poured a coffee, she could drink that same coffee all day long. It wasn't quite cold yet...Lee stuck his finger in the cup just to confirm his theory.

"Lee, take a seat, please," his mother said. Then, to the others, she explained, "Lee and I want to host a gathering here tonight so we can explain what has happened in Port Hope before our Cape family and friends hear it from the grapevine. It's always worse by then."

Looking at her son, who clearly wanted to 'get at it', Paradise said, "Lee, please go down to #8 Cape St Mary Road. I don't think Ben has returned yet, but a friend of his, I believe his name is Mike, is living there. You can share with them that Thomas was involved in a shoot-out with the two thugs who had murdered Clint, one of our partners. If they are free, ask them to join us around 5pm. I will fill everyone in and then we will share pizza...as many pizzas as my friends Waine and Denis can carry. Tell the boys we have the village of Cape St Mary covered, but if they know others who might know Thomas, like the staff at the grocery store and the post office, to invite them to join us here at 5 pm."

Eugenie had been sitting quietly. "Paradise, I know I'm interrupting, but could we make sure everyone who knew Pops, or knew about Pops, could join us in a toast to him over our pizza dinner? I'm not comfortable hosting something like a Celebration of Life, so if we do this tonight, I can concentrate exclusively on his funeral. Would that be okay? If I'm out of place, just tell me to sit still! I will understand. Paradise I will just add that if you wouldn't mind being the lead with the 'raise your glass' stuff, I would be very grateful."

"Oh, Paradise, wouldn't this be a great idea?" Wilmot said. "We could toast Pops quite easily, I think."

Paradise was all smiles. "It's a beautiful idea, Eugenie. We could ask a few to share their favourite 'Pops story' because, as we all know, everyone has one. We will do our 'Cape update' first. Thomas asked to be the one who gives it. We will add him on via a conference call first, because once the Pops related stories begin there will be no end until everyone has had a chance to share. Lee, you will oversee making that call happen."

"Are you still here?" Paradise ruffled her son's long hair and smiled as she motioned for Lee to get on with the task assigned to him. "Son, if Ben *is* home, ask him to drop in anytime to say hi. It would be nice to reconnect with him before we begin. I'm sure Hope will be on the conference call when your dad has concluded his report."

"Sounds like there might be something going on between Ben and my sister, so I can't wait to introduce myself to him. Maybe I'll ask what his intentions are."

Lee was laughing as he closed the door behind him, giving no one the opportunity to say anything more about this Lee and Hope thing...if it was a thing.

52: Suck it up

In Port Hope, the 'boys' were off to the hospital, where Thomas would have his wound and all its many staples attended to. He had been anxious just thinking about heading to this procedure, so both Jim and Hope suggested he had taken one for the team and could he please 'suck it up.' They made the suggestion in unison causing all three to break out in laughter.

While Thomas didn't really believe having been shot and then having staples removed was all that funny, he went along with the morning mood. They hadn't done much smiling or laughing in the last ten days, so he wasn't all that upset.

"I'll bring you and your brother a few staples as a souvenir, Hope," he said as he eased his still-sore body into the passenger seat of Jim's car.

Hope, at the front door, responded with, "We're good, but thanks." Then she lowered her voice and added, "Daddy, we are all so freaking proud of you and impressed with your mental recovery and healing powers."

The doctor who had stitched Thomas had warned him. "If you let the flesh heal itself on top of those staples, it won't be pretty taking them out." Thomas had not been able to unhear the doctor's warning.

After looking at the number of patients in the waiting room at the hospital, Jim leaned in and said, "Thomas, I can feel the flesh covering your staples as we sit here."

Both men chuckled, but the day was looking like a long one and Thomas appreciated the attempt at humour.

~

Hope was sitting at her computer, catching up on years of paper-work that Clint and Jim had not attended to. Invoices were all properly recorded, but details were missing. Who their client had been for each case, for example.

She wondered what experience Jim would bring to the team without Clint. She had logged at least five hours per day since her arrival and still could not see the end of the paper mess.

Both her dad and Jim had made the 'male' comment: "Never learned to type and even if I could, that computer would be foreign to me." Hope was not sure she believed Jim, but he was knee-deep in grief and she would give him all the rope he needed.

One day, though, she would sit Jim down to help her understand the blank dates in their schedules. On those days, nothing was posted regarding a client who might have hired them. However, on those same days, they deposited some of their largest amounts for a completed contract.

"What the hell happened on those days?" Hope was talking to herself. She picked that habit up from both her mother and Sydney. She did acknowledge that for at least a full week prior to those 'large deposit days' both Clint and Jim appeared to have been off the grid, so to speak. Not even a paper trail for one of the missing days.

Finally, as she entered the last 'job' Jim and Clint had recorded she wondered what on earth was keeping the boys. She wanted to 'pitch an idea' to them.

Sure enough, the boys were just through the door when Hope began her pitch. "I haven't talked to either of you about this because this idea came to me after you headed off to the hospital. I'll grab a couple of beers for you, so sit and get comfortable. Are *you* comfortable, dad? I'm sorry, I should have asked before I started my presentation."

Hope was laughing at herself, and her dad and Jim joined in. She could see that her dad had something to say. Maybe he was going to tell her about having his staples removed...something she had neglected to ask about when he came through the door.

She wasn't wrong. "Any takers for this bag of staples that accompanied me home from the hospital? There might be a bit of blood in the bag, but you can take it I believe." Thomas said this somewhat disingenuously.

"Hope," he continued, "for a second I thought you were my wife, always with a new idea as I walk through the door. All good ideas, but on occasion her timing has been a bit off."

Thomas drained his beer. "I know we have lots to work on here, but I need to talk with Paradise about the send-off for Pops. Hope, you and I might have to split up at this stage. Jim, we won't even consider leaving you alone, so let us talk with Paradise, and perhaps Eugenie if we can catch her, before we consider next steps."

53: What everyone really wants to know

Traffic on Cape St Mary road could never be described as 'heavy.' However, this day felt different. Everyone looked sombre but their expressions had nothing to do with traffic.

The invitation had come via a note, clearly in Paradise's handwriting and delivered by a handsome young man introducing himself as 'Lee.' Some did not know the young man and were a bit skeptical until they spoke with neighbours who pondered the idea that Lee might be Thomas and Paradise's son who had moved to Hawaii with his uncles over a decade ago. Could Lee be the real reason for the Cape party?

Literally everyone showed up at #548 at the appointed time.

Paradise had remained upstairs until everyone had arrived and found a seat. Lee then gave his mom a shout that the house was full to the rafters.

As Paradise navigated the stairs, she could feel the stares and the tension in the air, which she attributed to Lee's reappearance in the Cape as well as the absence of Thomas and Hope.

Lee turned things over to his mother, but he couldn't resist making a comment first. "Mom, the gang's all here, and anyone missing will get their comeuppance from me personally...guaranteed."

After giving her son a hug, Paradise smiled as she turned to face everyone. "How many of you recognized the tiny tot who entertained us with his young brain as the same young man who knocked on your door today? If there is any doubt, let me assure you that Lee is our son. He's home for a couple of months, during which time he hopes to check out a few universities in Nova Scotia."

Turning to Lee, Paradise added, "And now, my son, take your

seat and speak when you have something to say...or you might meet with your own comeuppance." She hoped this reference would bring a smile to everyone and perhaps lighten the moment. It did not.

Elise, who was friends with Paradise's mother a lifetime ago, was first to speak. "Paradise, please get directly to the point of this meeting. Since Lee knocked on our collective doors, the rumour mill has been working non-stop. Is Hope hurt? Is Thomas okay? Is someone dead? Are you unwell, Paradise? Please tell us why we are here and then we might be able to eat those pizzas Waine and Denis just walked in with."

Paradise took centre stage. Only those in the front row could see that she was standing on Pops' *soapbox*, as he had called it, but almost everyone could see her face. Some in the far corners near the mud room and the back door could hear, but could not see her. They were just happy to have made it inside the room. Others were still outside, wondering if they had been totally forgotten. One look through a window confirmed that the house was full and could not accommodate anyone else.

Paradise looked up from her notes, made eye contact with those directly in front of her, and began to speak with her neighbours. "We invited you here because we know rumours can travel very fast. So, let me answer those questions now."

She took a sip of her now very cold coffee, took a deep breath and shared everything. "Most of you know that Thomas and I have two partners in Ontario, Jim Taylor and Clint. During a gunfight last week Clint was shot. Thomas and Hope flew to Port Hope, Ontario immediately to be with Jim, who needed our help."

Hearing people murmuring to each other, Paradise said, "If you can't hold your question until I finish, I will take it now."

"Hi Paradise, did they get the shooter or is he still on the loose? I'm worried that Hope might be in danger."

Paradise recognized the voice right away, and turned to the man who had stood up. "Ben, it's wonderful to see you. Welcome home, young man. To answer your question, the man who murdered Clint died in the same shoot-out. I'll explain more as I go through my notes"

With a nod and a smile, Ben sat down and out of view.

Paradise, working hard to keep her voice from trembling, shared what she knew about the events in Port Hope, only leaving out personal details about the young boy whose death had precipitated the further violence. At times the noise level in the room got so high that she had to pause with her hand in the air until the crowd was ready to hear more.

The process was taking longer than she had thought it would, so Paradise suggested she could continue while everyone else ate pizza, and if someone could bring her a slice while everyone else lined up, she would eat quickly and then continue.

Before she concluded sharing where the paper plates could be located, and apologizing having forgotten to purchase plastic cutlery, her slice was delivered by the one and only Ben Champagne, who also delivered a message only Paradise could hear. "I am desperate to talk with Hope. Can I call her cell phone or do I need a PIU phone number?"

Paradise held one finger up to indicate, 'Hold that thought for a second while I inhale this pizza.'

When her mouth was empty, she said "Stick around because we are trying to connect Thomas via conference call. If we hear him, you know Hope will not be far behind."

As if on cue, a huge voice rang through the telephone lines. "This is Private Investigator Thomas Adams speaking, with apologies for being late. Blame it on Bell Canada, but not until this call ends. Bell might end our connection early if they get wind of a complaint. We have been able to listen to every word; we just couldn't comment. Jim is with me and there is someone else who would like to say hello."

"And this is Private Investigator Hope d'Entremont speaking. Oh. My. God. We were trying to visualize all of you, especially since mom told us the house was overflowing with our friends and neighbours. One more thing, and then I will take my place as second, make that third in command in our PIU offices in Port Hope. Ben, if you have the same phone number, I would like to call you as soon as this Cape event concludes."

"Ben just gave me a heads-up signal," Paradise said, "so clearly you have the correct number. He has been home from Paris for nearly twenty-four hours, and we have kept him busy all day." To her friends she said, "You have all been very patient so I will turn the phone over to you. Who wants to speak first?"

"I will. It's Elise speaking. Never in my entire life have I been part of a call like this. We can't see you. I sure do wish we could. We are all frantic with worry."

Thomas was quick to respond. "Elise, I recognized your voice. It makes me happy to know you are at our house with Paradise at a time like this. Do you have a specific question?"

"I do. We have heard so many rumours about this shooting and one is that you too were shot. God, I hope that's not true. Thomas, what can you tell us?"

"It's true that I have required a bit of medical attention, including surgery. I have been treated very well. I am 100% okay now."

A chorus of 'but?' questions rang out. Paradise waved her arms for silence, because Thomas was still speaking.

"Fast forward to what everyone really wants to know, yes, I was shot. In the leg. There will be a dandy scar I can show you once I get home."

When the next round of hubbub settled down, Thomas, with Hope's help, took them through the whole story of their adventure in Port Hope, adding details that Paradise had not mentioned or not even known about, so she was hanging on every word along with everyone else. She noticed, though, that Thomas's voice was getting hoarse, and realized that he must be exhausted.

When he next stopped to draw breath, she broke in. "We have almost run out of time for the conference call. I have one final question on behalf of everyone here: do you have any idea when one of you or both of you will be coming home?" Paradise realized how selfish that might sound, but before she could try to defend why she said what she said, PI Hope spoke up.

"Mom, Jim and I have been playing secretary with all the files here in the offices while Thomas was out killing the bad guy. I have an idea that I want to share with them, and after that we will be able to answer the 'when will we be home' question. Ben, I won't be able to call you right away because I need to share my idea with my partners. Don't go to sleep, though, because I'll call you as soon as I can."

~

"That was rude," Lee said to himself. He didn't know or care to know the phone company rules about conference calls but surely to God they could have given his sister a few extra minutes. He was a bit concerned that Hope might have been planning to say something sexy to Ben, though.

Suddenly he had a vision of Ben and his sister dancing to *Save the Last Dance for Me* at his parents' wedding. *And* his sister was wearing a slinky red dress, *and* he heard a few people ask if it was her 'slip.'

He hadn't understood all the chatter about his sister's dress then. A decade later, and he totally understands.

54: A better idea

Hope spoke from her heart as she looked at Jim and her father sitting facing her. She wasn't nervous, because what she was about to share wasn't earth-shattering or life-changing.

After taking a sip of her ginger ale, she said, "Let me start by admitting that I might have taken this a bit too far, but here goes, so hear me out and feel free to get up and move around, get yourself another beer—"

Thomas said, "Hope, we have talked about this. Please get right to the point or you're going to lose me. I'm that tired."

"Got it. Sorry, Dad and you're right. During my time here, with Jim's help, I have input all outstanding invoices, and then I converted the files to the system we use in the Cape, so we are all talking the same language. Secondly—and Jim, I hope you don't hate me for this—I consulted a local real estate agent and asked what this building might be worth. I also asked what we could rent it for. Jim, I can see your anger building, we are not kicking you out on the street. I think you should come home with us. Come to Cape St Mary. We are planning a renovation anyway, so our shared office will be a good size. We can find a cottage for you until you get settled. What do you think? Would you be willing to give it a try and fly back with us?"

Thomas spoke quickly. "Jim, this is news to me, too. But you must give the girl credit. It's something to think about, right? Maybe not today, but some day you might want to relocate."

Jim spoke only one word, and he didn't look at either Thomas or Hope. He kept his head down. "Today."

Hope walked over to him and put her head down in a mirror image to his stance. "Jim, do you mean you would like to pack things up and move home with us? We can take as much time as you need. My dad could go home without me."

"Today. I'm ready to leave the place where my partner was murdered, and the sooner the better. I feel like I'm going crazy just living in this place that we called home. I'm crawling out of my own skin and I'm afraid I'm going crazy." Jim sobbed as he spoke.

Thomas and Hope looked at each other and knew: one of them had to leave town in the morning with Jim. They would make it happen.

"Jim," Hope said, "I need to talk with my dad for just one minute. Don't move a muscle." Hope tried to make the moment light, but that didn't work out too well. Jim wasn't moving a muscle, but he wasn't in a joking mood either.

Outside of the room, with the door closed, Thomas said to her, "Hope, do you think you could take Jim home to the Cape? I could come a few days later after I sign some papers to get this building listed for sale."

"Not to one-up you, Daddy, but I believe I have a better idea. You and Jim need to fly together, and I will ask Ben to fly up here to help me. Mom can make up a room for Jim for a night or two. I'm twenty-five years old, not a kid. You can trust me here. Ben can keep me company while I get the best price possible for the building. Ben and I will pack up all of the files, although I might sift through them and discard duplicates. Private investigators are notoriously not good at paperwork of any kind. I've made a dent in it, but that's it so far."

"I don't disagree with anything you are saying. You're not my little girl any longer and I do trust you. I trust Ben as well. However...if he flies in while I am waiting to fly out at the airport, I might have a brief talk with Ben."

Hope could see her dad's smile grow until he laughed.

"Actually, Hope, I'm kind of kidding/not kidding, if you can understand my thought process. I don't want Ben or anyone else ever taking advantage of you...you are forever my 'little girl.'"

"I think I do understand. You go right ahead and have that talk with Ben. It will save me the cringe-worthy thought of you guys having that discussion later. I'll just say, 'Did my Dad have a talk with you about sex?' as soon as I see him, and before he gets into the car. That should make for a good opening line."

Still laughing, both PIs went back inside.

In the few minutes they had been outside something had drastically changed. Jim had a vacant stare on his face and wasn't blinking.

Hope quickly wiped the smile from her face, went over to Jim and bent down so that she was eye level with him. "I'm going to let my dad fill you in, Jim, but the great news is that my dad is taking you home to Cape St Mary tomorrow. I'm going upstairs to my room to make one quick call to coordinate a few things. Dad, over to you."

55: Nightcaps

Hope took the stairs two at a time, but spun around on the top step. She knew exactly what was wrong with Jim.

She ran back downstairs and pushed Thomas out of the way. "Get us some water, Dad, lots of water. Jim, listen to me. Look at me! *Look at me.* What have you taken? Did someone give you something so you wouldn't have dark thoughts? You used that expression the other day and I didn't recognize the meaning of what you were saying. Oh. My. God. Where is the empty bottle, Jim?"

She took a glass of water from Thomas. "Dad check, his room and the bathroom on this floor, and hurry. Then call 911. It will be helpful if the paramedics know what Jim has taken even before they arrive."

Turning back to Jim, Hope sat on the floor in front of him and took his hands. "This isn't the way, Jim. You are young and intelligent and loving and loyal, and I will not let you leave us just as we have a plan to get you out of here. Do you hear me? *Do you hear me, Jim?* You took something while dad and I were outside, correct?"

In barely a whisper Jim replied. "My doctor gave me...I didn't mean to take..."

Thomas was back. "Hope, it's Valium. The prescription is dated yesterday. 'Take two a day for five days.' The bottle is empty. Should I call 911 now?"

"Yes. Yes. Dial the number and put us on speaker."

Hope's medical training kicked in. Thomas helped her drag Jim into a cold shower, clothes and all, then stood by and watched.

"Jim," she said, "I need you to bend over and stick your fingers down your throat. I need you to bring up eight or nine of your

Valium tablets."

Jim didn't move or speak.

"I'm serious, Jim. I need you to make yourself gag and bring up the Valium. If you can't do it, open your mouth and I guarantee I will make you gag. Failing that, when the paramedics arrive, they will pump your stomach. I have seen that done my friend, and it's not pretty. Far more invasive than what I am asking you to do. Or let me help you. Come on, Jim. You could die from this overdose."

"I'll do it myself, thank you very much."

And, sure enough, he did.

The paramedics arrived in time to catch sight of the trio, all very cold and still standing in the shower. Jim was throwing up and Hope was catching what he produced and checking for Valium.

"Seven, eight nine: got 'em. Well done, Jim. I'm proud of you, now dad is going to stay in here with you while you have a hot shower. Then please join the boys and me in the office area. You okay with that, Dad?"

"Private investigator Hope d'Entremont, your 'dad', as you seem to want to call me, is happy to stay with Jim. But, with all due respect, you might need a shower yourself."

Hope ran from one shower to another and realized even her hair needed a bit of 'washing out'.

When she was done, she stepped out of the shower and into her favourite flannelette pj's. Was she confident enough to head back downstairs looking as if she was ready for bed?

'Damn right,' she whispered under her breath, before throwing on her dad's old bathrobe and joining the men. A lighthearted round of applause greeted her as she, in a rather unladylike entrance, jumped to the main floor, in full view of everyone, from three steps up the stairs. She would not have been embarrassed at all if she hadn't stumbled on her landing and fallen directly into the arms of one of the paramedics she had not yet met.

Not missing a beat, Hope said, "Well, aren't you just lovely, sir. I see you or someone else has brought dinner...pizza again and I love it. Is there any left, or am I too late?"

Thomas was on his feet, "We have your very favourite pizza

right here, and no one has dared touch it until we see how many slices are left when you are finished. Just kidding, we each had a slice from one of the boxes, and then we decided to wait for you. So, everyone dig in...Jim, you first! The experts here say you will be cleared to fly late tomorrow afternoon if we can get you to eat."

Turning to his daughter, Thomas went on, "Hope I have guaranteed the paramedics that walking along Mavillette Beach will be great therapy for Jim, and that he will never walk alone."

With tears in her eyes, Hope said to Jim, "I second that emotion."

"And that's about all the emotion we strong men of the paramedic bus can stand for one day," one of the paramedics said. "Jim, we will be back mid-morning with coffee and donuts. Just the right diet before you fly out of our great province to, according to Thomas, the greatest province in the country...Nova Scotia. My wife and I have been to Halifax many times. She's from Fairview, and the very next time we head east we will come all the way to Mavillette Beach. You have my word."

Hugs and thanks all around and, finally, Hope, Thomas and Jim were alone.

"Hope," Thomas said, "I booked our flights out for late tomorrow, which gives Ben time to catch a flight to Toronto, where you will have just dropped us off. Maybe not quite that smooth, but close enough. I promised him that the second we were on our own you would give him a call. So, off you go. But come back down for a night cap with us, honey."

"I will, and thanks for making all those arrangements."

Hope could see that Jim had something to say. As she approached him, with her arms open wide, he hugged her for the longest time. She could feel his sobs.

"Hope, *you saved my life tonight* and I will be forever grateful. I really didn't want to die, I swear. I wanted the pain to go away, and I kept forgetting whether I had taken a Valium. So, I took one more and one more and...I don't have to tell you how that story ended."

"Now you have me crying. I won't be on the phone long, so get that nightcap ready, Dad. One more thing Jim: let's not tell anyone in the Cape, or anywhere else, that I literally *asked* you to puke into my hands!"

In less than a minute Hope was lying across her bed, listening to Ben's phone ring, and ring, and ring.

She was kind of okay with him not being home. She knew she would be nervous when she first saw him, in less than twenty-four hours, but she would also be happy to be with him. They would have the privacy of the entire PIU offices. Hope thought the privacy would be perfect, given that the last time they spoke she was eighteen, just graduating from high school, running away from Ben and off to Halifax to begin her university education.

Thomas was still pouring the nightcaps when Hope returned. "With all due respect, Jim, should you be drinking?"

"Your dad and I talked about it, Hope. I likely won't have much of it because beer is my drink of choice, so please don't worry. The paramedics said my body will need a day or two to 'right-size' and it wouldn't be a bad thing for me to eat clean for a few days."

Jim took his glass from Thomas. "Before we do the nightcap thing, I just wanted to say how thankful I am that we are flying out of here tomorrow, Thomas. Thanks so much for making all the arrangements. I will settle with you later."

Hope thought there was a weakness in Jim's voice, but his body seemed strong, so she decided to go with that.

"There is nothing to settle," Thomas said. "PIU is paying the airfare."

Thomas raised his glass and nodded at Hope. "On your feet, boys. Here's to us...the three of us. What you went through before we arrived, Jim, is life-altering for all of us, but most of all for you. Dad and I will be with you every step of the way. Mom will, too, of course, We three are changed forever, so let's make it for all the right reasons. Thomas, Jim, I am proud to have been able to help in the smallest way. When you teach me how to shoot a gun, I can do more! Cheers!"

"Remind me to teach you how to make a brief, to the point and pleasurable for all toast Hope." Thomas was laughing.

Hope took it all in stride.

56: A beacon

Ben saw her immediately. Hope d'Entremont hadn't changed in the many years since he last saw her.

The last twenty-four hours had been a whirlwind from the moment Thomas had called and laid out the plan. Ben had agreed with it immediately. "Ben, to make this conversation even more personal, Hope is my little girl, and I'm asking you to keep her safe in every way until things are settled in Port Hope and you both return to Cape St Mary Road. Can you do that for me Ben?"

"Thomas, I will protect Hope with my life, today and always. I think you already know that." Ben couldn't hide the emotion in his voice.

And here she is, he thought, *standing right in front of me.*

"Hope, you are more beautiful at twenty-five than you were at eighteen, if that is even possible. When your father called me, I began packing as we talked. You remember how small my cottage is and how long the cord on my telephone is, so you can imagine me rushing around getting all tangled up in the cord as I packed everything I could think of in this backpack. I figure I can buy whatever I have forgotten. Port Hope does have stores, I assume?"

She rewarded him with a smile and that was good enough. They had nothing but time ahead of them.

Hope stepped even closer and threw her arms around him. "Oh. My. God, Ben. Thank you for coming. I didn't want to stay here alone, and my father was adamant that he would never let that happen anyway. And here you are! I'm so glad you were able to drop whatever you were doing to come and help me out for a few days. I will make things happen as fast as I can. I promise."

She took his hand and together they walked the airport concourse toward the exit.

"Hope, I was going out of my mind worrying about you. So, for the record, I am here of my own free will. Are we walking to Port Hope? Not complaining, but it seems that we have walked a long way already." Ben had promised Thomas he would keep the conversation light and that's what he was doing...for now.

"The entire village of Cape St Mary could fit into one of the many parking lots at this airport. We have about fifteen more minutes on the clock, at which time our limo will appear. Keep up because I'm driving, and I don't like to drive in the dark."

"I'll drive, Hope."

"No."

"Yes."

"No, final answer so no more discussion."

"Got it."

"Good."

"Hope, I have missed your one-word responses to any and all of my questions and I have missed our more serious discussions, too." Ben's last sentence fell flat, so the two walked in silence, no touching, no banter.

"Okay, see that brilliant red Jag just ahead of us?"

"Good lord, Hope, are you kidding me? Isn't that a bit too much car for you to drive, especially in a city like Toronto? Did you rent that car? I have trouble believing that your father would allow it. I know you're twenty-five but, for your own safety, why would Thomas ever agree to you driving a car with so much power?"

"We're actually in the small car just beside the Jag, but thanks for the vote of confidence in my driving skills, Benjamin." Hope wasn't really upset. "I set you up and you fell for it! I'll take that as a win, in case you're keeping track of who sets who up. And, thanks again for coming to help me close this place up, but one more reminder that I do *not* need a bodyguard."

"Busted. I will forever want to be your bodyguard, whether you need one or not and that is something I will never apologize for."

"Sure," was what Hope said out loud, but internally she wondered how much she could trust Ben. He seemed totally sincere, but all the things Doctor Scott had drilled into her head about not trusting men and not believing their one-liners and so on had been on her mind since she first thought of asking Ben to join her in Port Hope. However, knowing that Doctor Scott had never been married and possibly never had a date allowed Hope to not forget her mentor's comments, but to make her own decisions in life.

"I'll unlock your door for you. There you go, Benjie… Now buckle up. Do you need my help, honey?"

Ben was still laughing when Hope walked to her side of the car and got behind the wheel. "Calling me honey before we even get on the highway? Things are going my way, doll. This is going to be so much fun. You keep an eye on the road, and I'll keep an eye on you all the way to Port Hope."

"I need some fast food, so we'll be stopping about halfway to our destination. Are you hungry?" Hope had been so nervous she hadn't been able to eat all day. Now she was famished.

When Ben didn't answer, Hope looked over at her passenger, her bodyguard, her protector and there he was…fast asleep, head against the door.

"My God, I wish I had a camera," Hope whispered. How could anyone fall asleep that fast? Hope did remember Ben sharing that he had been up for more than twenty-four hours, so she would cut him some slack. She would have a bit of fun with this knowledge, though.

Some time later, as they pulled into the town of Port Hope, Hope knew where to find a fast-food take-out joint that was open twenty-four/seven. Deciding she would order two of everything if Ben didn't wake up on his own, she acknowledged she had no idea what his preferences for food were. They had so much to learn about each other.

Hope didn't *do kitchen,* but she placed a mean take-out order. She rolled the car window down and wondered if the chatter would wake her passenger up.

"Good evening and welcome, may I take your order?"

The young man behind the glass had opened his window and leaned out toward her. He seemed far too energetic for this time of the day, but this made Hope happy, thinking he would be sure to get her order right.

"You certainly may, and I will need two of everything I order."

"Sweet. I'm ready when you are."

"May I please have two cheeseburgers with bacon and all the trimmings on the side. I don't know what sleeping beauty beside me likes to put on his burgers, so I will let him dress his own burger, if ever he wakes up."

"Sweet."

"Two large orders of fries. Two orders of onion rings. Two high-test Cokes and two Canada Dry Ginger ales. Both drinks in bottles rather than cans, please."

"Will that be all, and how would you like to pay?"

"Cash."

"Sweet. Please drive through, park near the front door and we will bring your order out to you. That will be a total of $31.85, please, ma'am."

"Ma'am? Did you call me ma'am?"

Hope was talking to the wind. Buddy had taken her order and instantly closed the window.

When her order appeared, she handed over $40.00. "No change required, young man. Thank you."

"Sweet."

At least I change my one-word answers now and then, thought Hope as she drove to the PIU offices.

She didn't know much about men, but clearly they can sleep through anything! As she signalled and turned into the driveway Hope decided it was time to speak up.

"*Really?*" She nudged Ben just to make sure he wasn't dead.

"Oh no! I did not sleep through the entire road trip, and do I smell food?"

"*Now* you're awake? It's a good thing I didn't need you to keep me from dozing off. I have had a few sleepless nights myself with my PI partners. I believe I'm overtired from all the drama and all the trauma, but a good order of junk food will fix that."

'I'll make it up to you, Hope, I give you my word." Ben was

laughing at himself.

"So, I shouldn't take it personally?"

"God, no."

"Let's eat. Grab your bag from the back seat. I've got dinner."

By the time 'dinner was on the table' the grease from burgers and fries had stained the package it was in and the plastic place mats adorning the not-too-fancy table were dripping.

"Don't mind the décor, Ben...all the plastic will go. We have a real estate agent arriving at 0800 hours and your bedroom and bathroom are right through that door, in that corner behind you. Your quarters are on this level and mine are upstairs, so be up and ready before eight if you don't want to be caught with your pants down, so to speak."

"I'm going to ignore that expression for now because I made certain promises to your father."

"What else did my dad talk with you about?" Hope had finished her burger and every fry on her paper plate. She popped the tab on her first ginger ale and took a generous swig. Anything to keep her from looking at Ben.

How embarrassed she would be if her dad had broken his promise to keep her secret...who wants to be a twenty-five-year-old virgin? But she was 99.9% sure her father would not have shared her secret.

Hope decided she didn't want to hear Ben's answer. "I don't want to get into this tonight because I think we both need a good night's sleep. We can clean up in the morning. I'm up early and will get the coffee brewing. The real estate agent is coming strictly for a walk through, and she will return in a few days with a proposed selling price and a contract. She said that, over the years, she has had a few clients asking if she could let them know if ever we put our building on the market, so it might sell quickly."

"Like I said, I am here to help in any way I can. Now go to bed. I had a long nap while you drove here, as you will forever recall, so I've got a bit of unspent energy. Is it okay if I look through the files we are to eventually pack up and transport to the PIU offices in Cape St Mary? I'll clean the table up, too, and get rid of the garbage because we don't want the real estate agent to know about our junk food supper. Which I loved."

Hope said through a yawn, "Dad said you had become an accountant while back in Paris, so, yes, please, take a look at the files."

She was almost upstairs when she turned and sat on the top step with a bit of a nervous smile on her beautiful face.

"Ben, enjoying our burgers and greasy fries together, and looking at your face, I decided to share that in recent months I have felt more afloat than ever before, not feeling grounded at all, even lost at sea. Sitting here with you, and the ease with which we reconnected at the airport and began a conversation that we have both wanted to continue, I feel differently. Hard to believe, but I feel that perhaps, just perhaps, you will help me find my shore and I will no longer feel afloat and floundering. *We* will find our shore together. That sounds a bit touchy-feely and that's not me, sorry."

Hope was not sure she could say what she really wanted to say next, so she paused for a second to collect her thoughts.

"Hope *please* go to bed. It's late and, thanks to you, we have that early morning appointment. Good night, my love."

That last word hung in the air between them. To Hope, it was like a beacon.

"There's more," she said. "I'm not sure I know how to properly put my feelings in the right order, so forgive me if this is coming out all jumbled. It's just that... *I don't want you to think I have waited all these years just to be your girlfriend.*"

Then she jumped up, turned and walked into her room. Leaning on the door frame and slowly closing her bedroom door, Hope added in a whisper, "But I have. *Waited,* I mean."

Acknowledgements

To fans and supporters of *The Paradise Series,* I am humbled to have your continued support. I look for familiar faces commenting on each new title, and you never disappoint. I appreciate you so much. As long as you keep asking for more, I will continue to write.

Brenda Thompson, founder of Moose House Publications; Andrew Wetmore, editor; and Rebekah Wetmore, cover design: thank you for giving my books, both fiction and non-fiction, a home, a life, a 'look' and an audience.

Lexi Scott, thanks to you and to your parents for allowing me to use your photo as the source for the cover, although we have aged you several years for this book!

Thank you to Lexi's friend, Olive McKinnon, for snapping the photo that found a home on the cover of *Hope Afloat.*

About the author

Carol Ann Cole is a best-selling author and a professional speaker.

As the founder of the **Comfort Heart Initiative**, Carol Ann keeps her mother's memory alive with each tiny pewter heart sold.

To order your own Comfort Heart, visit

gifts-dev.cancer.ca/collections/under-100/products/comfort-heart-pendant

or call the Canadian Cancer Society at 1 888 939 3333.

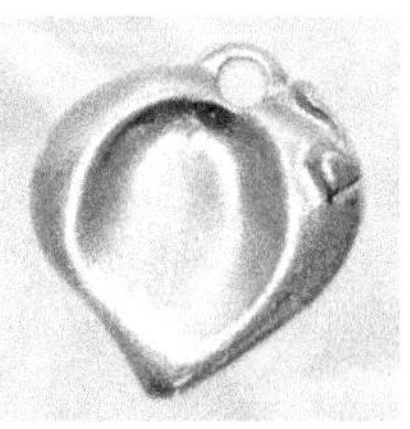

Carol Ann is a Member of the Order of Canada, and has received numerous other awards.

A believer in giving back to others, Carol Ann is a champion for those who need a helping hand.

Toronto is home, but Carol Ann can also be found in both Halifax and the beautiful Annapolis Valley in Nova Scotia, where she spent the first eighteen years of her life.